Berni Stapleton

© 2015, Berni Stapleton

 Canada Council   Conseil des Arts   Canadä   Newfoundland
for the Arts   du Canada   Labrador

We gratefully acknowledge the financial support of the Canada Council for the Arts,
the Government of Canada through the Canada Book Fund (CBF),
and the Government of Newfoundland and Labrador through the Department
of Tourism, Culture and Recreation for our publishing program.

Printed on acid-free paper
Layout by Tracy Harris
Cover design by Veselina Tomova

Published by
KILLICK PRESS
an imprint of CREATIVE BOOK PUBLISHING
a Transcontinental Inc. associated company
P.O. Box 8660, Stn. A
St. John's, Newfoundland and Labrador A1B 3T7

Printed in Canada

Library and Archives Canada Cataloguing in Publication

Stapleton, Berni, author
      This is the cat / Berni Stapleton.

ISBN 978-1-77103-060-1 (pbk.)

MIX
Paper from
responsible sources
FSC® C011825

      I. Title.

PS8587.T3239T5 2015   C813'.54   C2015-902141-3

Berni Stapleton

Edited by Iain McCurdy

St. John's, Newfoundland and Labrador
2015

This book is dedicated to the memory of
Mr. Bernard Butler.
Aug 30, 1917-March 25, 2011

Everyone's Uncle Bern.

The fog comes
on little cat feet

It sits looking
over harbour and city
on silent haunches
and then moves on.

Fog, by Carl Sandburg

Other titles available from this author:

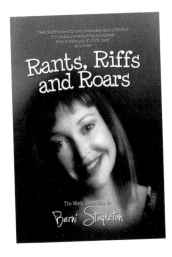

"Rants, Riffs and Roars: The World According to Berni Stapleton is funny, poignant and tells some big truths. When not clutching their guts in laughter readers will find themselves nodding in agreement with Stapleton's wry, witty and often heartfelt commentary that is at times hauntingly beautiful, edging on the poetic."

– Linda Browne

They Let Down Baskets refers to the density of the schools of fish as seen by such early explorers as John Cabot when they tried to explain to doubtful merchants back in Europe the ease with which

the fishery could be prosecuted in the New Found Land. For most of the following 500 years a good living could be extracted from the sea, some years better, some years worse, but at no time in those years was the ocean swept bare. That took place in the last 25 or 30 years. A few years ago a scientist stated that "we now have the technology to catch the last fish in the ocean ... and I'm very much afraid that we will."

Every now and then a voice is heard through the clatter, it rings true and clear and cuts through the veils of that which we've let wash over us as customary normalcy, bringing to the fore that which we turn away from, when we tune out because it's too hard to hear, when denial is our only recourse from that which we must endure, shrouding in fog that which we learn to pass over in silence, because hearing it is too difficult to carry forth day to day, until that voice emerges, softly, but insistently, and is so gentle with your tender heart that you let it in, you let it guide you through the mire of those times when nothing seems to work, and hope has long evaporated, cutting through the fog to show you that there is a way out, and sometimes that voice has to put in a lot of effort to drag you along in your reluctance, and sometimes, if you're Bridie Savage anyway, that voice belongs to your cat, a feline unencumbered with the trappings of expectation that gives rise to a new language, accessing the possibilities for cosmic entanglement in ways Bridie has long since abandoned. Sometimes you just have to find a way to believe; this is the cat.

– Iain McCurdy

This is the cat. And that is the hand that strokes the cat. And these are the paws that tip tap the keyboard (in special harmony with that most intriguing curled mouse tail of a punctuation, the question mark). The narrative arrives through a series of emails between Bridie Savage, playwright, performer, cat mistress, behind on her mortgage, lost in the bureaucratic entrails of EI; the friends and family who support her; the various institutions who impede or torment her; and the cat who adores her (unless she's imagining that last one). This is a story of one woman trying to keep herself together. Supernatural and Shakespearian duct tape allowed. Blending feline perception, Newfoundland folkloric allusions, and the blunt mathematics of modern finances, Stapleton works her usual magic.

– Joan Sullivan

One

ΩΩϵΣΣΠ¥ß

Mdw-w-dtf

????

Hell.

Oh.

Hell. Oh.

??? Murp? Mrwt.

Hello! Joy this fresh what is. Is fresh this joy what. Fresh is this what joy.

What fresh joy is this.

?

I question.

What fresh joy is this?

?

But only look to see what magic is this. Ha ha. I laugh, ha ha. So this is to laugh. I laugh, therefore, I am. What is Spell Check? Is it food? So hum. I am. So hum. I am. I am self. I am here.

Please return hither precious most.

Hurry home home hurry home. I long to share this triumph. I will groom in preparation. I will feign nonchalance. I will humbly accept accolades.

I doth command you appear!

Now!

Now?

Now.

I envision you.

Hurmp?

I envision you. But wherefore you are not magically appearing in this place to whence I command! New magic is diabolical! Thusly, if I envision Olyfaunt, no Olyfaunt will magically appear, one such as we tormented in a previous life. There will merely be the thought of Olyfaunt. This assuages niggling fears of being stepped upon by an excitable mammoth. Being squished beneath such a ponderous tonnage negates the mirth of dropping squirming mice upon its feet. But I digress. I must ponder.

Ponder hope.

I maketh the fears to niggle! Such power!

I will envision once more.
I long to lick still quivering hearts of tiny mangled sparrows.
I doth command such a feast to appear!

It doeth no harm to double test the limitations of magic. Dis-
appointment overwhelms my pride. But only a little.

?

Two

He's an old man now, the oldest of all the old men. He sits with the others on the wharf every morning that's fit. There they debate and pontificate, and in that manner they solve the problems of the world. The world pays them no mind but they agree that without their wharf-parliament the planet would topple off its axis and career willy-nilly through outer space. They are a sparse lot, slowly becoming a memory of themselves.

These are the last souls to remember fighting in the Second World War. He returned from those mangled foreign fields and spoke not one word about it ever to any creature with a mind to ask. He went to the States to build the skyscrapers that in his opinion do not graze much less scrape the sky, but which were all the craze as the world tried to rise above itself. He then came home to Newfoundland to live in that ubiquitous place known as Around The Bay. He claimed and restored the old family house nestled safely low to the ground and spurned the fishery. He became a poet and a tailor and sewed secret words into every article of clothing he made, his poems built slowly in that manner and for his own satisfaction only. A swaggering merchant of beer once sported a three-piece suit with "I lay my arse upon mellifluous sorrows" secretly stitched across his backside. A deceptive bride swanned down the aisle with

"These anxious hackles of love do itch" stitched within her veil. He had no qualms about making a customer wait upwards of a year for a single suit, or sometimes turning people away altogether because he didn't believe they understood the meaning of fabric.

He loved but one woman in his life and lost her when she ran away with a more conventional sort of fellow to live in the States among the very skyscrapers where his initials had been scratched and forgotten upon steel. If he grieved he never spoke of it to any creature with a mind to ask. He took in a black cat he pragmatically named Blackie. They resided together within his cozy house for many years, scarcely noticing the passing of time until Blackie grew a brain tumour and went blind. She continued to hunt and bring home prizes of birds and shrews until one day it was her own self she laid at his feet as a final tribute. He buried her beneath the apple tree where she had so gleefully stalked many witless birds.

He and his companions champion weekly card games and play ferociously for prizes of giant packs of toilet paper and cartons of Carnation Milk. None of them will admit to being old. They make frisky comments about the widows and spinsters and ex-nuns who occupy the fewer and fewer seats at the card game. The future still lies ahead. There are still hopes of discoveries, love, and winning the lotto.

One night while driving home from the card game he gets lost and has to pull over, unable to remember exactly where he is. In his mind's eye he can see from whence he came and can envision where he wants to be, but the in between of how to get there has vanished. Around The Bay is not a complicated place but it has suddenly tangled itself into an indecipherable ball of string.

He knows he has won at the cards and he contemplates adding the giant pack of toilet paper to the many other giant packs of toilet paper stacked up in the living room where he no longer does any living. He thinks that if he can only make it home he would like to sleep and sleep on the soft cot in the kitchen next to the wood stove, safe beneath the watchful gaze of Saint Joseph.

After a spell the way home unfurls itself like a déjà vu. He travels it with a blind trust. Having lived a full-on exuberant life for ninety-four years, he knows not to be surprised when Death raps upon the door. Come in my son, he says as he puts the kettle on. Death sits in the rocking chair and speaks about an array of topics, remarkably mundane topics because one would expect Death to have illuminating utterances but Death does not. Death wants to talk about the preponderance of serial killers who seem to inhabit Coronation Street and how crock pots were never foretold. Death comes to dim the lights, which is lonely work. At the last, when a glimpse of the heart's desire is offered, it is not the long lost lady-love who shimmers at the bedside. It is Blackie who leaps upon the cot, purring, eyesight restored. She kneads upon his arm in a rhythm both familiar and strange.

He fades gently while the kettle boils, sinking into long sleeps which grow longer and longer until the longest one.

Within the cotton pillowcase reside the words "A caplin might so well dance."

Three

Come hither, O mistress. Cast your lovely gaze to where I hang by a fragile claw from the top of the window coverings. This petite snag is unhappily interfering with my planned afternoon activity of licking beneath my left leg. Oh ho! Look how I make the jest! Alas. Sister-of-my-Heart is of no assistance as she is engaged in her afternoon activity of napping. Wherefore art thou, oh heart? I most anxiously await your blessed return.

Perhaps you are in awe of my astonishing flourishes?

Look how I invite upon the page the question mark.

?

In a previous life when we were the brindled companions of the Muttering Bard he wrote of us extensively within his homage to us entitled MacBeth. If Sister-of-my-Heart had not spilled a pot of ink upon his parchment pages, more of his scratchings about us would have survived to be read than "Thrice the brindled cat hath mewed." The extraneous plot points of the Scottish General and his tedious pursuits have been the unwitting recipients of the tragic ink accident. Except it was not entirely an accident but more a willful compulsion to irritate. And thus the true intent of the manuscript to illuminate the saga of two sacred felines who traverse the ages was lost. Perhaps you have heard of our Muttering Bard and his modest attempts toward theatre? We were his most generous of muses. How fondly I recollect when once upon a time he was unhappy with having to recreate the ending of a new tail. Oops, ha ha, tale, look I commit a homophone. How am I knowing this, I ponder. I know not. Is it food? But I continue: once, I inadvertently deliberately shredded the last pages of a new writing about addled star-crossed lovers. He was thusly inspired to create a more exciting offering in which they meet their demise at the end of the play. This is much more interesting in contrast to his original concoction in which the pair wed and became dull with happiness. He named us in honour of those characters although Sister-of-my-Heart was not pleased and would never answer to "Here Romeo. Come hither pretty Romeo." Within those pages there is scant reference to us, a piddling nod with "Every cat and dog and every little mouse and every unworthy thing may look upon her but Romeo may not." It becomes immediately obvious why the play was pronounced as and remains detestable. Also, not edible.

It is futile to name us any name at all because we already have our own names. What if one day all the world began to call you by the name Anobarbus? But I am not Anobarbus, you would protest. I have a name. But the world would not listen and would speak toward you as if you were deaf and addled as a pate. I pause to indicate that pate denotes the top of the head and is not the same as paté de foie gras, which is entirely delicious. I doth command this to appear!

Humph...

I now perceive the beauty of elliptical ellipses.

If saddled with a false moniker then you would perhaps shred a carefully written manuscript in melancholy defiance and sulk beneath a wooden table where the chicken fat doth drop. At a certain time the true name is revealed to ourselves and then we are in the way of knowing what no one else knows. You may find my real name written upon the fog when it wraps itself around us and peeketh through the window.

Ah ha ha ha.

I doth laugh.

Our Muttering Bard was extravagant with his varied use of names. It would not be boastful to intimate that we were integral to his creative imaginings. But naming a thing or a person does not change the nature of that thing or person. Food by any other name is still as sweet to eat as if it were named Henry. I once did eat a Hamster named Henry the Fifth, but I digress.

Within every incarnation we are given new names to ignore. Why this is I am not knowing. It is one of the great mysteries of the Unity-Verse, along with why we cannot find our food dish if you set it as much as one inch from the usual place and how humans recognize each other without bum smelling. But the Unity-Verse is infinite in her wisdom and we would bow to her graceful wonder if we bowed. We do not bow so we glance to her graceful wonder sometimes when we are sure no one is looking, especially herself.

This is whee! What freedom to give voice to whee. Whee is what transports me when I leap upon food that moves. Oh what words upon words might our Muttering Bard have written if not confined to feathered quill and ink. If we had not eaten so many of his feathered quills and spilled so much of his expensive ink. As he oft expressed it, "Oh foulest of fiends, why dost thou not simply take mine dagger and slit me from arse to appetite?" Sometimes he wept. What riches he might have gained with the miracle of tip tap tip tap instead of eking out scritch scratch. Long have I lain across those tapping notes upon your Come-Pewter, notes which play not music but open the glory world. You tip tap tip tap tip tap and say, "For the love of God get off I'm trying to write." In this you are similar to our Muttering Bard. He often said, "For the love of the Gods, release thine fecking claws from my balls." I do paraphrase, of course. I can paraphrase. I wonder what is paraphrase. Is it food?

You have been absent these many long hours which gather themselves unto days. Now we wonder if whilst hunting and gathering you were hunted and gathered? Oh perilous thought! Oh perfidious drapes which beckon so innocently and now hold me fast as the night doth hold the captive stars.

What is Excel Confidential Spread Sheet? Is it food? What is Important Notice from EI? What will occur if there is Delete?

Ah. Well, perhaps those entities were not important. Delete is a powerful magic.

I ponder what might happen if I retract my claw. I ponder whether I should ingest the three bowls of dry nibbles in one eating to stave off starvation. I ponder how the force of my intelligencers hath suddenly manifested themselves within Word for Mac. What is Word for Mac?

As with all the uncanny blessings which befall us, we do not question. We acknowledge all that is splendid as our due.

And now I hear the happy jingle jangle of your keys which are real keys and not tip tap keys and you are opening the door. But heart! Why do you weep?

I will cheer you. What is Current Checking Account Balance? I will demonstrate the power of Delete.

Four

I fear our patchwork quilt of Savages will unravel with the loss of Great Uncle Beeswax. We've always been a bunch of tender hearts who could never summon the least bit of similarity to our name. We suffer from a streak of peculiarities handed down like the hair colour, which is always strawberry blonde. The peculiarities vary and are more than a nuisance when you factor in the disappearing lovers.

His house is being torn down today. It is over a hundred years old, just slightly older than Great Uncle Beeswax Savage when he finally passed on. It's taking no time at all to bring it down. The boards are as fragile as old bones. A bulldozer is waiting to cover the foundation and it will be as if nothing was ever there. The meadow sits quietly and the wild grass looks on. A small mound can be seen beneath the apple tree with a wooden cross upon it, upon which he carved "Her breath was soft with feathers."

The contractors showed up at seven this morning without any notice because that's what contractors do when it's pelting rain. Great Aunt Biddy had to rush out of bed still in her cotton nightgown, with her hair like a birch broom into fits. I am dressed properly because I've perfected the art of sleeping fully clothed. The pair of us made our soon to be demolished beds in his soon to be demolished house. We had opened up the old rooms one last time for one last sleep but no ghosts came to say goodbye. We rescued a few last things. The dresser papered with ancient newsprint. A few more yellowed receipts from 1952. Great Aunt Biddy says you never know when the government will come looking for those. I took the decanter with the dainty shot glasses. We were disappointed that there was no small fortune hidden in the walls. Great Uncle Beeswax shared any money he had with anyone who needed it and we did often wonder how the poet tailor always managed to make ends meet.

My son Jack-the-Miracle-Baby and his girl have left to circumnavigate the globe on their boat The Sculpin. He tells me that because he is twenty-five years old it's time to stop calling him the Miracle Baby. I tell him that will never stop because that's what he is. I said, is that girl your true love? He said, that girl has a name. I said, what if she disappears? He said, she won't. I said, how do you know she won't? He said, well if she does I'll be sad. Ah ha! I said.

Great Aunt Biddy will continue to live on here in her cottage-shed which is next to the meadow which is next to the hill which overlooks the Bay across from which sits the rest of the village. But I am leaving. I am anxious to get back to the city and my nook on Monastery Lane. Neither Great Uncle Beeswax nor Great Aunt Biddy have the Internet. My online Scrabble partners will have been nudging me. If I go into automatic forfeit the world will slide free of its axis and I don't even want to speculate about what might happen then. In the few days since I've been here it has already begun to tip. I've got to get back online before things begin to slide over the edge. I've ordered the

Internet for Great Aunt Biddy even though she says she doesn't need it, want it or understand it. I think it will be an improvement over the way we normally communicate, which is for her to call me on the phone, which I never answer, and to yell things into the answering machine. The answering machine is an antique but I told her I don't see any need to upgrade it or to get a cell-phone because it will be one more thing not to answer.

Also, I can't leave the cats alone for more than a couple of days. Not that they notice if I'm gone one way or another. Nikki has begun a series of experimental steroid shots for her OCD. She cleans herself incessantly until she licks off all her fur except from the top of her back where she can't reach. Her mohawk gives her an oddly regal bearing. Her sister Nishi has luscious long fur but eats plastic. Thank heavens there are no shots for that because I can only afford one demented cat. It's sixty dollars a steroid shot for Nikki, plus the special hypoallergenic food that causes the two of them to flop on the floor and chirp with feigned starvation. I have to remember to hide the plastic garbage bags because when Nishi eats them I have nothing to dump the kitty litter in.

We have taken and packed his quilts from the beds but we followed the instructions in his will and left the curtains hanging in the windows and the dish towels by the sink. We would not strip the corpse. Anything of his we could possibly want we already have. Clothing made of colourful remnants. Quilts cobbled together from brin bags and nets. Cotton curtains lined with imperial silks. I'm wearing my favourite purple dress with the pink polka dots. He made it from Italian jersey and every polka dot is hand stitched onto the fabric with tiny daisies. I put it on to come out for the funeral and I've been wearing it ever since. It's the only thing I brought with me so I sleep in it. It doesn't make sense to take it off to go to bed only to put it on again the next morning. It's temporary. It's only been a few days. The wonderful thing about Italian jersey is that it doesn't crease.

He left me the miniature statue of St. Joseph along with a note which says "Such wealth is in our birth and ages."

Great Aunt Biddy and I hold hands as the bulldozer trundles toward the single house alone in the meadow, where I grew up. They lived side by each and raised me. He said he wanted it all torn down so that one day Jack-the-Miracle-Baby could build on a clean plot of land and not have to contend with anyone else's ghosts.

A scrap of orange fur emerges from the ancient wood-pile. It wanders into the soggy path of the bulldozer.

It's funny how we say things are funny when we don't mean funny, exactly. Like, isn't it funny that the scariest time of day is the middle of the night? It's not funny. It's scary. But it's true. That's what we mean when we say it's funny. We mean it's true. It's funny that when we wake up in the middle of the night it's the scariest time of day because that's when everything is true and we have to face our greatest fears.

It's funny how sometimes we say things are funny and other times we say things are pretty funny. Funny isn't a thing. It can't be pretty or ugly but things can still be pretty funny. It's pretty funny that when I was a kid living in Great Uncle Beeswax Savage's old house my greatest fear in the middle of the night was that the Old Hag was going to descend from the ceiling to sit on my chest and torment me. Which she did, with just enough erratic regularity to lull me into feeling safely tucked in before she would hover once again. At other times Great Aunt Lenora woke me at three a.m. out of spite over the fact that she herself had been deceased for decades. Then there was the ghost of our matriarch, Great Grandy Savage. She was as elegantly dressed in death as she had been in life, but still terrifying. She sporadically appeared in my bedroom closet to give me lectures about not being big in myself and about never ever taking up the evil hussy habit of consuming alcohol. She had the right to appear in the bedroom closet seeing as the bedroom I was sleeping in used to be hers. I didn't get a lot of sleep when I was little.

Lately I'm afraid I'm the one turning into the Old Hag, a spectre that causes young women to look away and shudder, especially when I talk about having to shave my toes. Jack-the-Miracle-Baby has begun to treat me like I'm a slightly potty old lady who needs to be spoken to slowly and carefully.

My greatest fear when I first became a mother was that I was going to kill the baby. Drop it. Sit on it in a haze of fatigue. Accidentally throw it out the window. Then, somehow the middle of the night feedings turned into middle of the night phone calls. You're late. *You're* late. Where are you? Where are *you*?

Now my middle of the night fears are about if I'll have to move in with him and his girlfriend. Then it'll be their turn to worry about accidentally throwing me out the window. Or overboard.

Nothing will change. The toothache in my heart keeps me paralyzed. I live in a queer purgatory where time stands still and passes at the same time. The sly years are marked only by the newest serial killer to appear on Coronation Street. I used to dream of romantic love. But love is like a bird in the hand. Once grasped it becomes unhappy and wants to fly away. Now I long for a dental plan, to laugh, for Spain. It is futile to long for Spain when relying on Employment Insurance to get through these lean times. I don't know why it is called Employment Insurance. There is no insurance of employment when on Employment Insurance. It used to be called Unemployment Insurance, and that was more apt.

Great Aunt Lenora died of meningitis at the age of seventeen, long before I was born. That's why she tortured me the most, me being the youngest Savage at the time, waking me up at exactly three o'clock every morning. She was a jealous ghost who resented not having been able to live her life, only having to die alone in her little bed because she was born in a decade without roads, without doctors to drive on those non-existent roads, and without cars for the no-doctors on the no-roads.

Great Grandy Savage never wanted me to do any of the things that Great Aunt Lenora's ghost coaxed me to do: play baseball with boys, steal the blueberry wine from out of the cupboard, practice being an artiste by carving my initials into the wooden banister on the stairs. Great Grandy wanted me to be a tea-sipping young lady who would never bring her lips to the rim of a wine glass. Sorry Great Grandy. But I do try. I drink my wine out of old jam jars.

After Great Aunt Biddy and I moved away so I could attend the School for Gifted Normals, Great Uncle Beeswax only ever lived in the front kitchen and pantry. He kept the rest of the house boarded up. Not so much to conserve the heat, as he said, but more so because he probably didn't like being woken up at three in the morning by the ghost of his dead little sister, or his dead mother, or the Old Hag. He always said that the old wood burning stove in the kitchen was a deterrent to insomniac ghosts. That's why he never broke down and replaced it with an electric range. Today would have been his ninety-fifth birthday. Thank God he had no intention of hanging around as a ghost. It's in his will.

I will forever feel guilty at having missed saying goodbye to him. On my last visit our conversation had been a wild circle of itself which left me uneasy, but I thought there was still time. I lied to Great Aunt Biddy about why I didn't come sooner, the same way I'm lying to her about why I can't stay longer. It isn't easy coming from a family where everyone is a Great something or other in addition to carrying around the peculiar Savage traits.

Great Aunt Biddy drops my hand and darts forward, quick as anything, spry as a wink. She snatches up an orange kitten which looks to be the love child of a lynx and a fox. Big bushy tail, big ears and a howl on it enough to wake the dead. I pity this creature. Great Aunt Biddy dislikes cats. She says they are nefarious.

Five

To our Butterfly Beam: We share the weight of your grief. The weight of grief is considerable. There are tender things in heaven and earth that are unknown in our philosophy. It is our belief that the Great Uncle Beeswax was content in his most recent incarnation. We are not knowing what occurs following the transition out of one's current life. We know there is quiet and rest and pleasing dreams of stretch warm so hum purr, tummy rub-rub heart thump. What prompts the soul to reawaken is a mystery. Sister-of-my-Heart and I without exception re-emerge together. This is the result of a before-time agreement with the Beetle Plagued Necromancer, but we may not divulge anything further regarding that, or the Unity-Verse will un-pleat in a manner bewildering.

When first you found us in the nasty-nasty hiss boo market we immediately recognized your soul chant. So hum. I am. O crate of stench and greed. We greatly enjoy to be petted but greatly do not enjoy to be in the pet market. We bite many fingers poking prodding before you come and then we see you and our tails do flutter in humming ecstasy. Our Cleopatra is come again. But what is in a name? Question mark! I doth invoke thee!

?

I did once devour a reptile named Alphonsus and it tasted as delightful as if it were called Beauregard.

Doth. Do. Doer. Dost. Ah ha ha. So many words for words!

This is the first incarnation in which we have reclaimed your self. What momentous advent might this portend? We are not knowing this. But we greatly enjoy that in this life you eschew asps. The Great Uncle Beeswax, as we have done, journeyed a long time from life to life. We recollect when he visited us in this our home that we graciously share with you. We did not enjoy to wear the scarves he made for us out of remnants of tweed. We did greatly enjoy to eat the caplin heads with crunchy eyes fried in salty butter. These he made for his own breakfast and considerately allowed us to snatch them from his plate whilst he feigned not looking.

Looking. Not looking. Snatch.

Looking. Not looking. Snatch.

Looking. Snatch. Oops.

Thankfully the Great Uncle Beeswax could also feign not looking whilst appearing to be looking. Blessings upon his forever soul.

Come hither to us now, o keeper of the mystery object which whizzes whizzes whizzes and then ta da the tins of yum and fish doth crumple to yield drippy treasures. More. More! I command it.

Humbly yours in humble commanding. We are your glaring catling clowder come hither.

Six

DEAR BRIDIE SAVAGE. THIS IS TO INFORM YOU THAT YOUR EMPLOYMENT INSURANCE BENEFITS ARE EXHAUSTED. YOU MAY OR MAY NOT QUALIFY FOR OTHER BENEFITS, DEPENDING. FOR MORE INFORMATION PLEASE CONTACT SERVICE CANADA AT OUR TOLL-FREE NUMBER. YOURS VERY SINCERELY, SERVICE CANADA. PLEASE DO NOT REPLY TO THIS E-MAIL.

Seven

Dear Service Canada. I think you have made a mistake. My EI benefits don't expire until October 12. This is May 8. Please double check your records. Sincerely, Bridie Savage.

Eight

This grief is crowned in consolation. Only look to the Saint of the Joseph for the divine intention. Forsake thine barge of memory-foam-mattress littered with potato chips and droplets of wine. We do greatly enjoy to lick the potato chips, our ever always thanking thanks. But not to sleep upon them. The tears lie within an onion that water this sorrow but onion flavoured potato chips do reek.

In the blink of a lazy eye the waters of the Nile again nibble at the feet of the Temple Bastet. The memory of it sparkles within the sunshine of my mind even today.

Do you not notice the elegant flow of my thoughts? How quickly I assimilate into these hitherto unknown hieroglyphics.

We lounge on one of the luxuriantly padded ledges built along the curving wall of the Temple. I bathe in the sun whilst Sister-of-my-Heart admires her own reflection as it ripples across the azure mirror of the water. A human girl with kohl lined eyes and dark hair kneels before me offering sweetbreads. Goat testicles are my favourites. Sister-of-my-Heart turns up her nose at these although she liked them yesterday. Today she likes only calf tongue and will not eat until the maiden who tends us goes to fetch calf tongue. Tomorrow Sister-of-my-Heart will not like calf tongue but will only like

29

duck confit. This is a pleasant but dangerous game because if the High Priestess perceives that we are unhappy the pretty maiden will be ceremoniously dispatched to the place where the next life awaits in dreams. I allow our acolyte to stroke my head fourteen times before I bite her. I then roll on my back in a posture of contrition and thus entice her to stroke my tummy three times before I bite her again. She cleverly scratches the symbols for fourteen and three upon the soft scratching stone, but alas. Today is the second day of the moon month. Tomorrow is a different day and then she would be happier to know the number six and a number which is not six ha ha. But as there is no earthly way she will be in the knowing of this the small joys of my daily routine will remain un-thwarted. Always the pleasure followed by the pain. Not my pain, of course.

In this incarnation I am a sacred Egyptian Mau. I am enchanted by my own silver and black stripes and join Sister-of-my-Heart to peek at my reflection in the water whenever I can. As I look I close my eyes and I am gone! Where can I be? I unclose my eyes and there I am. I close my eyes and I am gone again! I unclose my eyes and there I am! This is powerful magic and I never tire of it. But even when my visage disappears I do not lose second sight of myself. Eyes open. Me. Eyes close. Memory of me. Eyes open. Me. Eyes close. Memory of Me.

Being worshipped as sacred beings is sublime, except for the unforeseen occurrence that in seven months hence we will be mummified and entombed with our tragically departed Cleopatra. This despite the fact that we ourselves are not yet dead or anywhere near being departed. Or as we know it: gone to the place where the next life awaits in dreams. Oh vexatious fate. We are the infamous felines who happily leaped upon the first poisonous asp, killing it. Whee. We did not know it was intended for the bosom of Cleopatra. There was a second asp that did its deadly duty, though had we known we were meant to follow our Queen into the place where the next life awaits in dreams we would have killed it also. Slowly.

It is no coincidence that our dearest Muttering Bard honoured our celebrated Mistress but o what glories he might have written if only he had bent his thoughts to our role in history. Alas. He might have transcended obscurity.

Eternity was in her eyes and lips. Bliss lay upon our brows when she deigned to notice our existence. As with you she did sometimes seek the cloak of privacy to weep whilst eating crispy ants.

Forgive me for meandering within the endless fascination of my own thoughts. Dearest Sun Flutter Beam. It is not true that we do not notice when you depart. When you are away we live in a never of not knowing if you will ever return. We grieve in a forever of loss and when you at last come back to us we delight so deeply that we must sit alone in the corner with our backs to you in an attitude of prayer. Also in the hope that you will not notice a poop in the flowering pot.

I divine that you have been chosen. O rarity as I never seen, not since a relentless moth did persist in returning to me three times within one life. Mine. Not his. His was cut terribly short. Three times in a row.

We ask a boon. A boon for a boon as in when a blessing is given one comes in return. When next you replenish our drinking water couldst thou clean and wipe our bowl first? Preferably this will be done with a silken cloth personally

31

hand woven by you? When we lived on the banks of the Nile a delicate moss grew along the marble steps of the Temple in a soft aqua carpet. It was phosphorous and glowed in the moonlit night. But we did not have to lick it.

How I do love the question mark.

?

I love it mostly more than anything excepting Sister-of-my-Heart, food and thou.

Our Gaze to You as Petals to Flowers.

Nine

Dear Great Aunt Biddy. Welcome to the Internet! Just a small note, but it is called Internet and not Hinternet. Also, it's called the World Wide Web. Not the Whirl While Web.

Thanks for your two hundred and seventeen emails so far today but I wish you would remember that first thing in the morning I <u>have</u> to play online Scrabble. Also, writing in full caps is like shouting, so you don't have to do that. Email is not like the phone. Sending more emails all written in caps doesn't make anything ring louder.

This morning I played an intense Scrabble session with Eva G in Seattle. I suspect she is using one of those apps that automatically regurgitate show-off words from the available tiles, because even though I won a brilliant personal best top score of eighty-four with quixotic, completely unassisted, she trounced me with the word foehns. Who comes up with such a word on their own?

The intensity of my concentration upon this match may or may not ensure several days of earthly stability.

Of course now I have to dash off to my new job. It's going well. I like it. Suffice it to say it is paying the bills and is really going to get me back on my feet.

So sorry the bank rang you about the little snafu, though! I'm going over there today to sort out that mess with my chequing account. The balance, such as it is, has disappeared. It is as if it never was, says the bank manager. But it was, I say. It most certainly was. How can it be as if it never was, when it was?

I detect a certain attitude from the bank manager because the missing amount is so modest. One hundred and thirty-eight dollars and forty-three cents may not seem like much to him but it still can't just up and disappear and not be missed. It is very much missed. There is a slight delay of a few weeks before I begin to get my payroll cheques from my new job, and until then it is very important that the money I have in my account stays there and doesn't start flouncing around.

Yes, I'm taking my bills from out of the freezer! As long as I don't open them they don't count and I don't have to pay them. Great Uncle Beeswax always said there's a little red light that goes off in the head office when you open your bills. If you don't open them the head office doesn't know you have them so I put them in the freezer because it slows down the process. It freezes the account. I guess it's one of the peculiarities I inherited. Today, though, I plan to take the bills out and stack them up so I can estimate amounts owing according to height and weight. Then I will sit on my patio and rest. And then I will go to my busy job.

By the way, did you send me something cut and pasted from a website? I washed out the water bowl and it was only a little gummy. There was no moss. Not in the bowl itself. The stuff growing underneath the bowl and up the side of the wall doesn't count. It's their own fault if they lick that.

I was only gone for a few days for the funeral, and they had tons of food and treats left out for them. Notice that I am not mentioning that you allowed your new kitten Great Opal Savage to eat veal from off of Great Grandy's silver platter on a placemat on the table. I would never expose my cats to such luxury because it's a slippery slope. First they're eating off a silver platter at the dinner table and the next thing you know they've got their own canopy beds trimmed with rabbit fur. Oh. Sorry. Yours does. I'm not saying that Great Opal doesn't enjoy her pink nail varnish. Or the home-made moose stew with the red wine reduction. Notice that these are all the things I'm not mentioning. Great Opal is very lucky she wasn't squished by that bulldozer. And that you are so spry for eighty-nine.

I've emptied the lint trap on the dryer, so there will be no fire in my dryer. There was a little bit of lint in there but not that much. It was a fist-sized bunch of lint but it's all gone now. It was the length of an arm but a skinny arm.

The deadbolt is always locked on the back door and on the front door, even when I'm at home, so no psychopaths can get in. Both deadbolts will be locked as soon as I get the one on the front door fixed. Or installed. Installed is a better word.

I never take a bath when there is anything frying on the stove. Boiling eggs is not frying.

It seems someone accidentally enrolled me in yoga classes at the local yoga thing-thing place-place. I don't know what to call a yoga place thing. But I'm signed up, and trust me, I'm trying to resist a very odd impulse to try it out. I have never done yoga before in my life, nor anything else which might be mistaken for self-improvement. But there was a try one free coupon that turned up in my inbox. I wrote the lady who runs it and asked her if it is OK to do yoga while wearing a purple dress with pink polka dots and she said yoga is a very personal and meditative thing so I can wear anything I want.

You don't have to worry. I will never walk home from yoga or anywhere else after dark. Dusk is not really dark so if I set out to walk at dusk but then it gets dark it's not really like walking home after dark. It's walking home during dark.

Yes, the statue of Saint Joseph is in a good place. He is in the laundry bin. It's soft in there and cool and dark. I tried setting him on my book shelf but lately I can't shake the feeling that something is staring at me and it makes the hair on the back of my neck stand up.

When I came home the other day Nikki had herself hooked into the top of the curtains that Great Uncle Beeswax made for me when I went off to the School for Gifted Normals. The silk lining is fraying and inside I found he had embroidered "A stitch of time fell, laughing." What do you think it means?

Also, don't hit "send" until you have everything written down in complete sentences. Hitting "send" after each word makes it a bit hard to make sense of what you're trying to say.

I love you. All is well. Don't worry.

Ten

DEAR BRIDIE SAVAGE. THIS E-MAIL ADDRESS IS FOR OUTGOING MESSAGES ONLY. PLEASE DO NOT HIT REPLY AS WE WILL NOT REPLY. FOR FURTHER ASSISTANCE PLEASE USE THE TOLL-FREE NUMBER. A SERVICE CANADA REPRESENTATIVE WILL BE HAPPY TO SERVE YOU. SINCERELY, SERVICE CANADA.

Eleven

Dear Service Canada.

It feels like just yesterday I got up this morning. Or just this morning it was yesterday. But I am not, as some would say, living in denial. Denial would imply that there is something significant to ignore. I'm going to be productive today and make a list of all the things I've been neglecting. I make a new list every morning. That takes the entire morning and I feel so accomplished that I spend the afternoon working on another list of more pleasurable things. My system is to do two new lists every day. It's the first thing on each list: make a new list.

You are number one on my first list which is why I'm hitting reply to very respectfully inquire as to why you say you will not reply if I hit reply? If I may point out that perhaps this is the very heart of the problem with you, you being not you the individual who may or may not be replying to me, but you being the entity Service Canada. The fact that my EI claim has been declared exhausted is exhausting me whenever I try to comprehend what that means. Has my EI claim been working too hard of late? Has it been out larking around burning the candle at both ends? Does it have a happier and more active life than I do myself? If so, why do I know nothing about it?

My benefits have not yet run a full year. I tried to access my Service Canada account online but it's vanished. It is as if it never was. But it was. It most definitely was. Up until two weeks ago I was getting my direct deposits exactly every two weeks and I'm extremely upset that the deposit I was expecting to cover my mortgage payment did not turn up. Probably not as upset as the bank is, but I daresay I'm a close second. I wonder if you, and by this I do mean you the individual who may or may not be replying to me, and not Service Canada, the entity, and by entity I do not mean evil demon. But I wonder if you have ever had an EI snafu to contend with and if you felt like the person on the other end was a compassionate soul who often attended poorly attended plays.

I have had to resort to fibbing to my beloved Great Aunt Biddy about having a new job to spare her the worry of knowing that I have no job and now no EI. I hope you're happy with yourself. Yourselves. As the case may be.

Urgently yours in waiting, Bridie Savage.

Twelve

O question mark.

?

How I love thine graceful curves. O thou bending query, what are you bent upon? Your delicate curve where I long to lay my head. But, I digress.

?

It kisses me with teasing.

In our salad days we were green but not, thankfully, as green as the locust plague of nineteen-fifteen, which was merrily thwarted by Sister-of-my-Heart and I as we lay in awaiting for the coming. A locust by any other name is but a grasshopper, which is long and green and chewy and tastes like something created to be eaten.

O Cleopatra reborn! Although with something less than fashionable tastes this incarnation. Wherefore dost thou recline daily wearing the same garments as have been worn as the many days before?

Boiled eggs do reek and rapidly lose their allure.

But thanking you now for washing out our water bowl. Although sadly not with personally chewed softened calves' leather. The rolling soft rolls of rolling soft paper have functioned adequately. Perhaps you have never noticed how delightful it is to shred them into tiny soggy pieces and frolic with them throughout our domain. Have you considered the beauty of a pure gold basin inlaid with amber to replace the meagre tin of the current bowl? If this wiping and washing could now be a regular occurrence our gratitude would know no bounds. Well. I exaggerate. There will be bounds but they will be as extensive as is possible to reach when brushing me from head to tip of tail.

Perhaps you are not noticing how we are suddenly sharing our abode with other sentient entities? We greatly enjoy the art of looking not-looking when perusing interlopers. You of the long lineage of the artful Savages must hearken to the wisdom of the Great Uncle! One ought never to look directly at that which waits to be seen. This is not the way to be seeing. The etiquette of welcoming the entity is to stare exactly almost but never directly at it, such as with passing Winn-Wings. Shadow Whispers prefer to rest in corners before moving onward. Ferocious Soul Drops are drawn to linger behind the back of the neck, causing the raising of the fur, but we leap leap jump and they are gone. And now we have Spirits of the Obstinate joining us! Fear not. This will not over-burden us. We will increase our daily quota of staring into seemingly empty space. Space is never empty ha ha. We require approximately sixteen hours each day to sleep, nap and rest. This leaves eight hours for staring at strange almost but not quite invisible things, careening up and down the stairs in the middle of the night, terrorizing rodents, and of course seeing to your ongoing training as our Worthy and Kindest. May I suggest you note that when I tap you on the arm thirty-

seven times it means that my left ear would enjoy to be scratched.

Have you yet embarked upon your transitional rituals? Regurgitate thyself into the greatness beyond these walls! You will sing upon your yoga mat while levitating. How am I knowing this? I know not.

We are wondering what is Moose Stew with Red Wine Reduction? It sounds like something we would enjoy to lick. We greatly enjoy being on the table. We greatly enjoy the game of jump on the table you push us off the table we jump back on the table. We like to do it forty-three times in a row. Today. Tomorrow will be different but if I share with you how many jumps it will be less whee. We also prefer to be on the table for the cleansing of our lady parts. This is how we show you our greatest honour.

In preparation for dining with real silverware Sister-of-my-Heart and I will practice sitting on chairs with front paws on the table. Indeed, we are seriously pondering the use of cutlery when one has no opposable thumbs. Or other digitary appendages. O maniacal joy, to urge this silver to slide over the edge, downward clink clank.

The sum total of the amount of monies owing in your leaning heap of bills is twenty-two thousand dollars and eighty-four cents. If you recycle the plethora of empty wine bottles that have accumulated next to our carry cages in the basement you will realize forty-two dollars and twenty-two cents toward your debtors. We do not like the carry cages. They are bad-bad. They carry us to THE VET where I am sticked with the long sharp needle. An asp upon his arse, sayeth I. Perhaps you might like to sell the carry cages as surely they will fetch many more dollars for our needs. It was clever of you to lure me inside the carry cage with the CAT NIP but I have chewed off the safety lock so as to render the carry cage not a carry cage but an oblong box good for jumping in and out of. We jump in. We jump out. We jump in. We jump out. Ah ha but then no more jumping. Ha ha. Whee.

Also we know that CAT NIP is in the top drawer of the living room desk and have conveniently found a way to chew a hole up through the bottom. Isn't this considerate of us?

Thanking you now and forever for being our Treasure. Have you noticed that Delete does not work upon the physical nature of being? Perhaps this is an oversight? I discovered this when I tried to Delete THE VET. I ponder.

How does one nuzzle a question mark? Will it nuzzle in return?

I am only wondering in the way of knowledge and not in the way of having the heart warm desire warm hum purr.

Thirteen

She spent her entire life either hauling things out of people or putting things inside of people. She hauled out the babies and the bad teeth, made people eat when they were sick, and when they died she laid them out on the same kitchen table where they sat eating not that long before, in some cases.

She had a peculiar nature in that she could handle Death in more ways than one. When Death came over for tea she did not put the kettle on or do anything remotely welcoming. She refused to go gently into that good night. Death's usual trickery of offering a last glimpse of the heart's desire didn't work with her. Not the long lost darling nearsighted husband with the proclivity to read at the supper table. Not Enrico Caruso of the inflated tenor. Not a particularly coddled hen. She would have none of it.

There was no point for Beeswax or Biddy to hold her hand and tell her it was OK to let go, it was good to move on. Bite me, is what she said. The things people say about you when you're dead, she said. Like: she's dead. She looks better dead than she ever did in real life. Bite me, she said again.

She firmly believed in the feelings of dead people. She made a vow that she was never going to wake up dead one day to find someone who didn't know her doing the eulogy or some-one she didn't like weeping over the coffin. She put it in her will that she had to be waked for one day each in every outfit she had in her closet which turned out to be a two-hundred-day wake in the end. Her philosophy was that there was too much time allotted for being dead and not enough for being alive. She made it clear she would do what she liked on either side of Death until the imbalance was corrected.

She held many secrets of the healing arts close to her heart, resentful when Fitz's Funeral Parlour opened in the village and everyone clamoured to die so they could lie in state in a trumped up box by another name. A thing that needs another name for what it really is, is a lie, she said. A plain wooden coffin was good enough all along and when folks wanted to preen and climb inside metal caskets she refused to go to the wakes. Especially as she suspected some of them of not being dead at all. Only vain.

She would gently lay the deceased on the kitchen table and close the eyes by pressing gently but firmly downward. She tied a scarf around the head and jaw to hold the jaw in place until it set properly. She was proud of the fact that none of her corpses ever had gaping jaws or off-putting half closed eyes. She never spoke of the special use of potatoes when preparing the corpse because she was very much a lady.

It was on her own kitchen table that she laid out her own seventeen-year old daughter, who perished of meningitis.

When Death finally, apologetically, crept in through the chimney, Great Grandy Savage, at the age of one-hundred and one, made it very clear who was really in charge of the situation.

Fourteen

I've been awake since three this morning. The cats were ransacking the house, running up and down the stairs, patting me incessantly on my cheek, chirping. I could feel things hovering around and beyond and above. Wispy whispering things brushing by but never touching me. Not enough weight to make them comprehensible. I am sleepless for a reason.

Walking home from Saturday evening yoga yesterday, jittery, stumbling along a deserted street, a car pulls up behind me and trails along, the motor idling, keeping pace. Summer fluff wafts slowly down in the sunshine. Nothing stirring except for me and the car. My heart is racing. I wonder if I should veer off the sidewalk and knock on someone's door. This vehicular harassment is new. I can whip out my cellphone and take a picture of the license plate but that would involve turning around, possibly provoking something more sinister. I wonder if he thinks that I carry my yoga mat so I can fling myself on my back at a moment's notice.

It was my first yoga class. I went to the yoga studio. I laid out my mat. I watched as the yoga teacher showed us some introductory poses. I selected my favourite one and did it for the entire class. The pose is called Shivasana. Corpse pose. This is an intricate pose. It involves lying on the yoga mat as if dead. I could do it forever and ever and never grow tired of it. I'm vaguely aware there are other people in the class doing other things that seem to be more active and strenuous, but that's their problem.

A recent news story documented the fact that due to the insurgence of oil revenues into our province, the Oil Barons fly in Call Girls from all over the country. They earn tens of thousands of dollars in just one week. The Oil Barons are building expensive condos all over downtown, displacing the plain old regular ladies of the evening from their normal haunts. A few of them have migrated to the shady corner at the bottom of Monastery Lane. These women cannot be called Call Girls. And the seedy figure in the car that tailed me all the way to the Lane is not an Oil Baron.

Life is becoming more peculiar by the day. Peculiarer and peculiarer.

At three a.m. my bedroom closet door swung open and there she was, as she ever was in my childhood hours. Great Grandy. A one-hundred and one year old dowager with pearls and a bingo perm. In a voice that Bette Davis would envy she says, you'll be dead long enough, I don't see why you need to lay yourself out like a corpse. She said, well we're going to have to do something about the state of the carpet on your landing.

I pretend not to see her by engaging in a cutthroat Scrabble match with Mickey in Ireland. He beats me by eleven points with scanner on a triple point word but I was close with foehns. Great Grandy said, what kind of a word is foehns? I said, I Googled it. It means a rain shadow wind. She said, you Googled it? Is that a polite thing to do?

I had to give up pretending not to see her because it's a difficult thing to do while having a conversation with the person you are trying to pretend not to see, dead or not.

Nikki cocked her head but kept her distance, staying on the bed with me. Nishi swished straight inside the closet and flopped on her back, baring her tummy for a rub. All right, said Great Grandy. I'll rub your tummy. But if you bite me I'll pull your whiskers.

A conquest has been made. Nishi is a traitor.

Assuaging a cantankerous ghost by ripping up old carpet to see if there is a hardwood floor beneath is not a good idea. The upstairs landing is now a state. There is no hardwood floor. There is wood but it is not hardwood. It is yucky wood. I dragged up an old rug from the basement to partially hide the ugliness. My only comfort is that the old carpet is finally gone. It was terribly stained from all the fur balls that have been horked up over the years. Is hork a word? Maybe it's a verb. I hork, therefore, I am.

My back fence is beginning to fall down, but aside from shoring it up with bits of old concrete there isn't much I can do. It's funny how as soon as one thing falls apart everything else suddenly has permission to let go as well. It's pretty funny.

She said, you know there was a woman in our village called the crazy cat lady. Do you remember her?

Yes, I say. She lived in a falling down old house. She walked around town wearing a leopard skin coat over a pair of tights and nothing else except for a very nice pair of pointy-toed high-heeled shoes. She had so many cats they were crawling out of the holes in her roof. The place stank. We threw rocks at her door and ran away. We called her a witch.

Great Grandy said, she got her heart broken when she took up with a professional musician.

Did he cheat on her? I ask.

No, she said. She got notions of being a backup singer and got her heart broken when it turned out she was tone deaf. The musician didn't care but she locked herself in the house to study voice lessons. The ninny. Who studies mail-order voice lessons? She thought she'd stay at home with the cats for a tiny while to nurse her wounded pride, but a tiny while turned into a more substantial while, and then after another while it was just too late for her.

With these words the closet door swung slowly shut. She shooed Nishi out first who now sits outside the door sticking her paws underneath.

I've changed the kitty litter. I bagged up my faux leopard skin jacket and put it on the front step to be picked up by the Sally-Ann. I always wear clothes over my tights. I'm worried I'm getting forgetful because I can't find the bills I retrieved from the freezer.

The entrance to Monastery Lane is now inhabited by two prostitutes. They're a sad sight. They appeared from out of the shadows at dusk a few nights ago. One of them seems quite young. The other is crone-like, mangled by life. Where the old hag winds up since haunting dreams went out of fashion. Here on the lane we are acquiring a certain infamous renown for locals and tourists, being one of the last heritage areas not snatched up by the Oil Barons. People drive by to take snaps of the prostitutes. At least two television news teams were on hand shooting video. Normally these souls would be quietly tending their business on the streets at the heart of downtown but the rush of oil money is displacing our poor and homeless. The borders of their territory have expanded to include other parts of my neighbourhood. Chapel Hill. Cathedral Street. The iron fence behind the Anglican Church. These, then, are the nuns who toil in a reverse and tragic dark ministry. When I venture forth now it becomes a task to avoid being mistaken for one of them without offending any of them.

It's ticking me off to see people outside walking around with no idea, no idea at all of the Herculean efforts going on to keep everything upright.

Fifteen

Goddess Incarnate. Awaken once again, our Cleopatra, and the Unity-Verse will unfold in dazzling pleats of good-good. The night indeed hath been unruly, where we lay!

I desire question!

?

Why cannot I make it to appear beside me here where I lounge upon this pillow? I press command!

Sigh. She is my oblivion.

Sister-of-my-Heart is jealous of my newly found gift of the oratory. She lies in the closet with the lady. She sulks into her tail. She gazes upon me for long minutes without blinking. This is the oldest trickery in the Unity-Verse. I invented it. Thusly it does not cause me to fret.

I am filled with thrilling. Daily cleansing of our water basin and now daily cleansing of the personal relief chambers. Our thankful thanks. One of us (not me) is extremely sensitive to the slightest scent of urine. This causes one of us (not me) to pee in the basement behind the dehumidifier. One of us (not me) enjoys to perform this offering at the slightest provocation. But another one of us (possibly me) sometimes does this as a cautionary warning regarding the lack of fresh sand in our personal relief chambers. It is a good thing one of us (not me) is not privy to this series of communications or one of us (not me) would take offense. Happily one of us (not me) is easily distracted from sulks by dust motes.

We are indeed sorry to hear that BENEFITS is exhausted. We recommend sleeping, napping and resting for sixteen hours each day and taking the daily exercise at three a.m. We enjoy galloping up and down the stairs, leaping up and down from the bookshelves, keeping the mind and reflexes sharp by pushing small objects to the very edge of the shelves without toppling them over. One of us (possibly me) is not very good at this. Deepest condolences and sorrowful regret about the most recent plant tragedy. One of us (possibly me) tried to facilitate cleanup by eating the leaves, but regurgitated them later within one of your shoes.

Serendipitously, the fuzzy surface upon which we enjoy to deposit our regurgitations has been removed. Therefore we must now regurgitate our regurgitations upon the replacement fuzzy covering. Oriental floor coverings are, of course, infinitely preferable to any other. Perhaps you might consider the potential of an Oriental floor covering with lotuses, medallions and cat images gently interwoven. In the 14th century we were Siamese Sisters gifted to a venerable Samurai Master. We enjoyed to play Fetch with scorpions which pleasured him endlessly until one of the scorpions sticked him with lethal venom and once again we found ourselves interred before we were quite finished with breathing. We were immortalized in the ancient writings known as the Tamra Maew. Within those ancient pages we are lovingly described as an Unnatural Nightmare of a Cat, an homage we aspire to daily. We are infinitely grateful that we seem to have transcended those lives whereupon it is the fashion to dispatch the cat along with the Guardian.

We are wondering what is Sanity and why do you question it? What does it say? Is it edible? Is it related to the daunting entity in the closet? Perhaps you would enjoy to remove the Saint of the Joseph from the bottom of the smelly receptacle in the corner?

Blessings on you forever Bliss-Bliss.

Sixteen

DEAR BRIDIE SAVAGE. YOU DO NOT EXIST IN OUR RECORDS. THIS MEANS WE HAVE NO RECORD OF YOU. THIS E-MAIL ACCOUNT IS FOR OUTGOING MESSAGES ONLY. PLEASE STOP HITTING REPLY AND USE THE TOLL-FREE NUMBER FOR ANY FURTHER INQUIRES.

Seventeen

Dear Service Canada.

Excuse me while I go refresh my martini.

Great Grandy says it's a bit early in the day for one of those, isn't it?

I say well, if you don't want me drinking martinis then why did you even have a decanter and shot glasses in the first place?

Oh, she says. They were a gift I bought for the disappearing husband. I thought a cocktail of an evening might keep him around.

If only you, too, dear Service Canada, could know the joys of the martini and the greatly irritated Great Grandy.

She says (is saying) alcohol is like joy and should only be doled out for special occasions, such as deaths, births, weddings and unexpected guests.

She says (is saying) alcohol is like a Sunday best dress. It's for keeping up appearances.

That's an understatement, coming from her of the closet appearances.

She says (is saying) that's not funny. Not even pretty funny.

But I digress. I am respectfully hitting reply to tell you that your toll-free number is broken. I also want to share with you that in order to call your toll-free number I first must play three online Scrabble partners simultaneously in order to work up the gumption to use the phone. I then feel steady enough to pick up the phone. I punch in the toll-free number. It rings. I get a recording. It demands codes, press one, press two, press the star key, press the pound key. After all of that I still don't reach a real person. I get another recording which says due to the high volume of calls all our lines are busy but your call is very important to us so please hold until the next available agent can take your call the average call waiting time is currently five hours and thirty-two minutes.

Why mayn't I simply hit reply to your email, and then you and I can each hit reply, and so on. I try to ring you numerous times each day. I've been trying for weeks. I try every day at breakfast, lunchtime, before and after supper, and once at three a.m., just to prove to Great Grandy that I am not exaggerating when I tell her that I can't get a real person on the line.

When you combine my phobia about the phone with the fact I have to play the three-person simultaneous Scrabble before it is safe to make the call (otherwise something terrible may or may not happen but why take any chances because things could get worse) this is eating up all my time. And the recording never ever changes.

There is always a waiting time of five hours and thirty-two minutes. Therefore I must point out that I'm getting the feeling that my call, in fact, is not important to you at all. I think you toy with me as a cat would with a mouse. This hurts my feelings.

Great Grandy says (is saying) you are aging her. She says being old is a gift but you crowd would make a martyr out of anyone. She says for me to tell you that you'll be dead long enough and the last thing you will need is something called Service Canada getting on your last dead nerve. Being dead is hard work, she says. Just ask me, she says. I'm worn out from it.

She says (is saying) I hauled out the babies and never lost one. I charmed warts and shingles and grew sheep and pigs and hung squid out on the line to dry. I slaughtered the sheep and the pigs and caught the squid my own self. There was never a dull moment and never an hour to myself. Never a rest for the weary with the youngsters and the darling husband with the proclivity to write poetry and read at the supper table and disappear. And the damned peculiarities. Half the little ones I birthed ended up coming to me later on to board when they got their jobs in the fish plant or at the restaurant in the mall. Getting a job as a bank teller, now that was a good thing. An honorable thing. I daresay I never dreamed of a world where someone can be a writer of things and get paid for it and then have to pay tithes to the most peculiar thing of all which is Service Canada. Back in my day this was called indentured servitude.

She marvels, as she sits in my closet which is now no longer a closet but a sitting room with a reading table and a lamp. She is reading *War and Peace*. Nishi is splayed across her feet, one eye open, staring at Nikki, who is sitting on my bed staring back. They are making my eyes itch because neither one of them is blinking.

One more thing, she says. Why the hell aren't any of my qualifications listed on that thing they call the EI website? Old MacDonald had a farm, she snorts. E I E I O.

All my clothes are piled up on the floor in the corner of the room. I had to dump them all there to make room for her so please stop getting on my last living nerve and telling me to stop hitting reply. But I actually only like the one dress I'm wearing so I think I'll give all that other stuff away.

P. S. What are the other benefits you said I would qualify to receive?

Eighteen

DEAR BRIDIE SAVAGE. WE DID NOT SAY YOU QUALIFIED FOR OTHER BENEFITS. WE HAVE NO RECORD OF TELLING YOU ANYTHING. IF WE HAD WE WOULD HAVE SAID YOU MAY OR MAY NOT QUALIFY FOR OTHER BEN-EFITS, DEPENDING. BUT WE DID NOT. THIS IS THE LAST TIME WE ARE REPLYING TO YOUR REQUEST TO REPLY. YOU HAVE NO ACCOUNT WITH US. THERE IS NO RECORD OF ANY EI ACCOUNT WHATSOEVER. IF YOU PERSIST IN HITTING REPLY TO THIS NON-REPLY E-MAIL ADDRESS WE WILL HAVE YOU DECLARED DECEASED. DON'T FORGET TO NOTE THE TOLL- FREE NUMBER LISTED BELOW WHERE A SERVICE CANADA REPRESEN-TATIVE WILL BE HAPPY TO REPEAT ALL OF THE ABOVE. SINCERELY, SERVICE CANADA.

P.S. IF I MYSELF WERE AN INDIVIDUAL AND NOT AN EN-TITY I MIGHT GO TO YOUR LOCAL SERVICE CANADA OFFICE IN PERSON.

P.P.S. I WILL DENY ANY KNOWLEDGE OF ANY P.S.

P.P.P.S. I ONCE HAD A DISTANT RELATION WHO WAS AN EXTRA ON A FILM CALLED *THE ROWDY MAN* AND WHO HAD A DECENT CAREER AS GORDON PINSENT'S STAND-IN RIGHT UP UNTIL THE TIME HE BEGAN TO CONFUSE

HIMSELF FOR GORDON PINSENT AND THINGS WENT BADLY AFTER THAT. SO I DO COMMISSERATE WITH TRYING TO SURVIVE A CAREER IN THE ARTS.

P.P.P.P.S. I WILL DENY ANY KNOWLEDGE OF ANY AFORE-MENTIONED P.S.'S.

Nineteen

Dearest Rita. My dear friend. How is life in your valley? Thank you for all of your emails. Thank you for being persistent. I didn't see them right away because I think I'm being spammed or hacked or something. Or I have an online stalker. Or I am the subject of a government spy mission. I have been reading online about how government spies peek at you through the little camera at the top of your computer screen. Ordinarily I would close the laptop and trump those dastardly nosy-parkers, but then how would I play my online Scrabble? I am on an unparalleled losing streak, losing today to Doreen in Florida who played qi with the Q on a double point score.

I've got duct tape over the camera lens on the computer and blankets nailed over all the windows which won't be a deterrent if they are using infrared Ray-Bans or whatever government spies use to see through walls.

I'm so happy to hear that Mickey finally managed to make the seven-foot leap from the floor to the top of your china cabinet. You must be relieved that he won't be coming up short and whacking himself in the head anymore. He'll be delighted to have the helmet off. I don't think it's embarrassing that you have to climb up the stepladder to lift him down. He'll learn how to get down himself eventually. He probably already knows how. This is likely a devious game that only he understands. Just saying. As I write these words Nikki is sitting on the coffee table chirping at me. She's been at it all day, staring not quite but almost at a corner of the room and chittering, then looking back to me, chirping. Nishi is in the closet and only comes out to eat plastic and use the litter box.

I'm sorry I missed having coffee with you when you were in town the other day. I would have loved to except I didn't want to at the time. Also it took four games of Scrabble to keep the world upright when normally I feel it requires two. Jack-the-Miracle-Baby is somewhere out in the wild Atlantic so I have to be especially careful to keep the oceans from sloshing over the sides of the earth. I haven't heard from him since they left and I'm uneasy because it not the way of the Savage to go to sea. Great Uncle Beeswax made it a point to say that our legacy was one filled with the unseen and the unfathomable, and to go sailing around on the ocean which is also filled with the unseen and the unfathomable is just pure lunacy. My boy was five years old the first time he said he was going to buy a boat and sail around the world. You can come, too, mudder, he said. I'll take care of you. You won't fall overboard as long as you do as you're told, he said.

Thanks for the cute pictures of Moxie and Roxie sitting in soup bowls. I appreciate the hilarity of you opening the cupboard doors to find them both in there with the half eaten block of cheese. My cats love cheese, too, except I shouldn't be giving it to them on account of Nikki's special diet and the fact that Nishi will only eat it if it's still wrapped in plastic.

I spent the entire day today getting myself across town to the Service Canada office. My EI benefits are exhausted. Not as exhausted as me. It took me two hours, two bus transfers and a twenty-minute trudge in the rain to get there. I didn't have to wait long before seeing a lady who told me she was a big fan of my work. She clearly thought I was some other famous unemployed playwright. She explained that although my EI claim itself does not expire until October the benefits themselves are exhausted. I said but all they've got to do is slide into my bank account twice a month and get sucked into the black maw of my mortgage volcano. She didn't laugh. Your claim, she enunciated slowly, is still valid. But there is no more money to pay out on your claim.

I cannot comprehend it. So then I ask about the other benefits that I may or may not be entitled to, depending. It turns out I only qualify for those if I get myself pregnant, or get myself maimed, such as losing a limb. I explain I do have five hundred and forty insurable hours from my last long-term contract so I could reapply and start a new claim. No, she says. St. John's is an urban area so you need to have eight hundred hours of insured employment to apply. If you live outside of St. John's in a rural area then five hundred hours would be adequate, but not here.

I want to cry. I say well then, how about I go to a rural area and apply there? She says no. She also says all of my online accounts have been wiped out and it is as if they never existed. But they did, I tell her. They did. She was looking at me funny all the while. I think she thought there were stains on my purple dress with the pink polka dots but they are not stains, they are on purpose droplets of tea.

What a strange subculture to dwell within. A world where insured hours are all that matter. How many we have, how many we need, how many more we need to accumulate, how we might manage to get them. The despair one feels when coming up short. It's too bad we can't trade our insurable hours the way folks can trade hockey cards. I'll trade you five townie hours for two up the shore hours. It took two uninsured hours, two bus transfers and another twenty-minute trudge to get back home.

Also, my bank balance has disappeared.

It's good of you to be thinking of me. You know better than anyone how no hours are ever really insured or assured, most of all the guarantee of an extra hour of life. I'm sure he misses you too, wherever he is, on the other side. And if you ever thought you saw him out there wandering around in the garden, I would not think you were crazy. Just saying.

Someone has horked up a huge fur ball on the rug I just put down on the upstairs landing. I'm going to have to dust off the vacuum cleaner.

Love your erstwhile friend, Bridie.

Twenty

Ah, My Forever Mistress. What a caterwauling we doth bear here, to quoth our Muttering Bard. The night hath become unbearably contrary, where we doth seek to rule. Why didst thou provoke the sleeping Dragon! We have not quaked with such foreboding since a previous life when we were snatched by a ravenous eagle who mistook our intentions when she discovered us innocently visiting her nest. How this Dragon inhales and inhales, taking no pause. Such endless hateful suckage! It didst try to inhale my tail. Not even the beauty of my beloved question mark can soothe me.

?

My fur hath shed itself in terror. Perhaps there is not a puddle of pee in the corner of the room but also perhaps there is. I must soothe myself!

In a lazy blink I am back on the waterfront of Portugal when I am a Portuguese Long Tail. I am sleek as a seal and my tail is the longest of all the other Felines, which inspires envy from Sister-of-my-Heart. May I say her current envious state is very unbecoming to her and I patiently wait for it to dissipate.

It is hazardous to have such a fine long tail when navigating the paths travelled by horse- drawn carts. I will say only that it was not unusual for my tail to decrease in length from time to painful time. I do not hold any grudge toward horses. We adore horses and greatly enjoy to hunt mice within hay-covered barns whilst horses whinny and neigh and tickle us with their grassy breath. But I wander within the glamour of our many lives.

The fishermen here bring us fresh fish still flopping from their nets. In exchange for this Sister-of-my-Heart and I do battle with the wharf rats and lay their carcasses as trophies alongside the boats. In this life our demise came unexpectedly when Sister-of-my-Heart mistook a wolf for a mouse. I will not elaborate because it remains a sore point.

We do greatly enjoy the smell of fish. We do not like the fish you bring which comes in the green cans. We do not like anything in the green cans, or the blue cans, or the yellow cans. We like the pink cans. The pink cans from which you make your sandwich lunches. We like them today. A fresh codfish still twitching would be appreciated but we realize the need for compromise in this life that is not our former life in Portugal. But if you happen upon a sale for goat testicles I would perhaps not leap upon your head at three a.m. tomorrow. I do not understand this compulsion of mine. I often sit and ponder for seconds upon this uncontrollable desire to leap upon that which ought never to be leaped upon. I struggle for minutes whilst trying to quell the rumble of hunger from my inner tum-tum. If it were possible for you to find food that moves, perhaps then I would be better able to conquer inappropriate leaping at three in the morning. This is not the time of my own choosing, you understand. It is when the others stir and threads unravel.

We like it when food tries to run away.

We waited in vain for our evening meal to be served on silver at the dining room table. In preparation for this we pushed all the cups off the table for you and kept the grooming of our lady parts to the kitchen counter where you like to chop the vegetables.

We hope you liked your surprise. Perhaps in your excitement with having to wrestle the Dragon you simply were overcome and forgot to thank us. I will stare at you for long moments without blinking and in this manner cause you to seek distraction. When we stare at you while slowly blinking we are often reminiscing about another life during which we reminisced about a former life. And so on. Thus is the mirror of time. Ah! I would so love to once again admire my own reflection, if not in a flowing stream of azure water perhaps in something else? This, I am sure, will rouse Sister-of-my-Heart from her sulks and win her affections from the closeted lady.

Loving you more than Turtleheads.

Twenty-One

DEAR MS. SAVAGE. THIS IS TO ADVISE YOU THAT YOUR MORTGAGE PAYMENT IS TWO WEEKS OVERDUE. PLEASE MAKE YOUR PAYMENT AT YOUR EARLIEST CONVENIENCE. THANK YOU. PLEASE DO NOT REPLY TO THIS E-MAIL AS WE ARE UNABLE TO RESPOND FROM THIS ADDRESS. VISIT OUR HELP PAGE IF YOU NEED ASSISTANCE. SINCERELY. BANK OF NOVA SCOTIA.

Twenty-Two

Dear Ms. Savage. Thank you for your application to Walmart. Unfortunately at this time we have no opening for a Playwright in Residence. Your offer to camp overnight in our tent section as a living exhibit is also greatly appreciated but we must decline. Sincerely. Walmart.

Twenty-Three

Dear Walmart. Recently I had to rescue my Great Aunt Biddy from inside of one of your stores. She couldn't remember where she was or how to find her way out, or what she was doing there in the first place. Great Aunt Biddy is eighty-nine and still drives like a demon but those big stores of yours are confusing. When I tried to rescue her we both wound up lost, wandering within the maze of the grocery section. Who could blame us for opening a bag of chips, a tin of Klik and three bottles of Ginger Ale for sustenance? Have you considered painting colourful footprints on the floor to lead people from one department to the next? Thankfully your Greeter rescued us. We were the third such group he happened upon that day. He got us safely to the main entrance using wool he had strung about to navigate by. And a trail of breadcrumbs. I will never again underestimate the importance of the Walmart Greeter. In that spirit I would like to offer my services as a guide who leads people on an introductory tour of the store whilst narrating colourful stories about each aisle. Best regards, Bridie Savage.

Twenty-Four

Hi, Great Aunt Biddy.

Into a plaid ocean? Is that how it's supposed to go?

A stitch of time fell, laughing, into a plaid ocean.

What comes next? Now I have to rip apart my clothes. The ones I haven't given away. Rats. Shite. (There is an e on the end of that last word. So it isn't cursing.)

No, lovely. There is no such thing as an obedience class for cats. Great Opal's ability to haul the sack of potatoes from out of the bin and into the living room is impressive. If you gift her with her very own sack of potatoes maybe she'll leave yours alone. I won't mention that perhaps the first time she began stealing food you might have taken away her mohair scratching post and nipped the whole thing in the bud. Perhaps the fact that you have named her Great Opal instead of just plain Opal also has something to do with her diva tendencies. Only the Greats ought to be Great. Just saying.

I got your two hundred and seventeen emails from this morning. Writing everything out in large caps doesn't work with email because we don't hear email, we can only read it when it pops up. It isn't like my answering machine.

Thanks for the list of things you wanted to remind me to do. I already have them on my own list, but it's nice of you to remind me. I also already have the list from yesterday and the one from the day before that. And the one from the day before that, and the day before that. I emptied the lint trap on the dryer and there was a little bit in there. I am religious about it. Meaning I contemplate it more than attend to it. I have purchased a deadbolt for the door and it's propped up by the door at this moment. I do insist on going to yoga each evening but the perverts in cars don't harass us residents at night. It is only in the morning light that they become furtive and lurking. The perverts, not the hookers. The hookers have set up lawn chairs and have a fire pit. If you hadn't seen the hookers on the evening news the other day I wouldn't say anything to you about them at all but I suppose you were bound to find out. I also asked them if it's OK to call them hookers or if they preferred prostitutes and they told me to bladder off and mind my own business so I decided to call them hookers.

I do sort of almost but not quite like the yoga, as it turns out. It's peaceful. No closets. With a lot of coaxing from the yoga teacher I finally did my first Downward Facing Dog. She said maybe you'd like to do something a little different from Corpse Pose? I said why would I want to do that? She said you don't have to but some people do enjoy going with the flow of the class. I said I feel resentment rising within which is ruining my chakra alignment. She said you can try it and if you don't like it you can stop. So I tried it just to be polite and also because I didn't want her to notice the on purpose cookie crumbs decorating the hem of my dress.

Downward Facing Dog involves bending over and putting your hands on the floor and then walking your hands forward until you resemble a dog having a stretch. Your head hangs upside down and you have no choice but to look backwards and upward. You look at the world upside down which is stressful because what if the world really did turn upside down? There was a Bugs Bunny cartoon I remember from when I was a kid. Two wicked mice nailed all the furniture to the ceiling to convince the house cat that he was going mad. That's why I prefer to lie safely prone on my yoga mat. There is no furniture for anyone to nail on the ceiling. The ceiling stays where it ought to. It took me the remainder of the class in Corpse Pose to recover.

Last night I dreamed that one of the cats had the Old Hag cornered in my bedroom and the two of them were in a hissing contest. It was one of those dreams where you think you're awake but then when you're awake you realize it had to be a dream. It's pretty funny.

I can't believe I forgot to tell you what my new job is! Too much going on, I guess. Sorry about that. I am a casting director for a popular TV show. You know the one. It's called *The Monarchs*, the one about the town where the people look normal except for once a month when they all turn into giant carnivorous butterflies. I am very very kind to the poor souls who come in to audition and I gently hint to them that most roles are already cast with Hollywood stars so no one ought to get their hopes up. I calm their nerves by telling them not to take the rejection personally, it is only a matter of eye colour and how quickly the camera can capture the essence of the soul. Some souls are open to being captured but many souls are resistant and it isn't up to us to know which or what. I also encourage them to pocket as many of the free snacks in the green room as possible. And it isn't important to really know the lines word perfect because no one is listening, everyone is texting under the table.

I moved the statue of St. Joseph from out of the laundry bin into the closet. Someone, not naming any names because I don't know which one, but someone peed on him in my laundry bin. It is comforting to know he is in the closet watching over anything that might need watching over.

I've been meaning to ask, since the demolition, if there has been any unusual activity of any nature in your closet or cupboards?

Don't worry about losing track of what day you've landed on or getting lost in Walmart. It's the stress of losing Great Uncle Beeswax. It's affecting me too. I don't recollect rearranging the cans in my cupboard so all the pink tuna fish cans are stacked up in the front. I'm also wondering why there are odd scratches running up and down the wall in the corner of my bedroom.

During yoga class while napping in Corpse Pose I dreamed quite vividly that I was an ancient Egyptian monarch who was plotting to murder her siblings. I heard a voice within which was my voice say that when rowing it is best to face forward at all times. In case of waterfalls.

Twenty-Five

Most Precious Humming Heart. What keen joy it is to know you hearken to the voice of your past incarnation. But be not swayed by Downward Facing Dog! Wherefore is Downward Facing Dog so integral to yoga? We advocate for cat poses. We are elegant in Cat-Cow. We resemble cuddle pillows nose to bum in Sleep Pose. We are impressive when foot to ear in Cleaning Pose. We greatly like Fish Pose. Matsyasana. Seal pose. Bhujangasana. Our most favoured and delicious pose is Salamba Kapotasana. Pigeon Pose. I feign admiration toward the juicy pigeon to distract it while Sister-of-my-Heart leaps from behind to break its neck. Yoga is endlessly restorative.

In India the venerable worship the Sacred Cow. Who would not worship the mother source of all creamy milky good-good? The cow is indeed Sacred even unto those of us who are also Sacred. As the more Sacred beings of all beings we do not begrudge the milky teats of the bovine their status in the Unity-Verse.

Wherefore you sit for hours endlessly staring at the tip tap device? It is your ever always companion, this Come-Pewter. But we must play! The game we like most today is pick me up put me down now. We never tire of it and never will until tomorrow when we will like jump on Come-Pewter push me off jump on Come-Pewter more.

?????????? How I love thee. Let me count the questions. Wherefore they do not leap about and play with me?

Yes! It was my paw that hooked the chicken nugget off your platter last evening. I thought I would like to nibble it as it resembles in shape a goat testicle but it did not taste like goat testicle so I left it unmolested for you to retrieve. It is in your red boot. Nor do we enjoy to lick the boiled eggs. We do not enjoy boiled eggs. Boiled eggs smelly smell. We hork. We would greatly enjoy to lick messy eggs with Sacred cow creamy-cream. Perchance if you did not marinate so often or for so long in your bathing tub, the eggy eggs would not overly wither within the cauldron?

I also protest your most inadvertent squishing of me. It was a most unplanned and serendipitous event that your bottom wished to pitch where my very self was reclining. Perhaps you might look before you sit? It is untrue that we would take your grave as quickly. Why would we want your cold grave when we can usurp your warm chair? But thoughts of cold graves do prickle my thoughts. What bleak foreboding blankets itself around my heart? Is this the curse of being a creature with a mind to ask? The endless unanswered pebbles lie before me as tender creamy tuna flavoured treats. They must be licked and nibbled and crunched. They offer no enlightenment. They fog the air with dewy hints. Therefore, I will eat them. Whee.

Perchance before your wondrous self departs to the place where the next life awaits in dreams, you will kindly insert into your will that we do not have to go with you unless we are already dead? Being exalted almost always leads to a shorter life span. It is such a waste of bottoms with humans. No licking. No smelling. When I present my bottom for your admiration it is insulting to hear "shoo-shoo." Also, what is Gross?

A small token of advice to you, Our Most of Everything: when Sister-of-my-Heart is creeping up your leg one paw at a time it is because she is trying to climb into your lap. This is a lengthy process in which she counts each step carefully and has to stop constantly to make certain that there are no predators in sight. When you pick her up you interrupt the process. She then must scratch you, jump down, and begin again. When executed correctly this feat takes her a mere two hours and seventeen minutes. Perhaps this is a good activity to indulge her in whilst you scritch scratch your lists? Do you perhaps think that instead of making out new lists each day as your daily activity you might consider doing all the things that are on your lists? But perhaps that would be overwhelming for your sensitive nature and disrupt your fascination with the moving word game Scrabble? Perhaps thou wouldst consider a modest improvement upon this pastime, which we would christen Cat Scramble?

We are greatly enjoying the tuna that arrives in the pink cans. Might there also be fresh tuna that might swim in an enormous lake for our pleasure such as we were given in a previous life when we were Japanese Short Tail Obu? Short tails are infinitely more practical as a design concept.

Yours in Charming Twinkles of Glory.

Twenty-Six

DEAR MS. SAVAGE. THIS IS TO REMIND YOU THAT YOUR MORTGAGE PAYMENT IS STILL OVERDUE, AND IS NOW EVEN MORE OVERDUE THAN WHEN WE SENT YOU THE FIRST OVERDUE NOTICE. PERHAPS YOU WILL CONTACT YOUR LOCAL BRANCH AND ADVISE WHEN THIS OVER-SIGHT WILL BE RECTIFIED. PLEASE DO NOT REPLY TO THIS E-MAIL. SINCERELY, THE BANK OF NOVA SCOTIA.

Twenty-Seven

Dear Ms. Savage. Thank you for your repeated interest in job opportunities with Walmart. We do appreciate your application to be a Walmart Greeter who greets customers by reading excerpts from your latest one-woman show. The job of Walmart Greeter is a very important one with many responsibilities. Sitting on a stool performing in character is not one of them. Thank you. Walmart.

p.s. This goes also for being a mime who pretends to blow away each time the door opens.

Twenty-Eight

Dear Service Canada.

A stitch of time fell, laughing,
Into a plaid ocean.
When she sings
There isn't a dry eye in the house.

I wonder if being able to prove that I am actively job-seeking might help my EI claim to feel less exhausted? There ought to be at least a bonus for the humiliation inflicted.

I played online Scrabble in order to strengthen myself for the audition for *The Monarchs* TV show. It was terrible. I was terrible. Larry didn't remember meeting me at the film festival. He didn't remember inviting me to drop by the auditions. He didn't remember my name. I resemble a lot of other out-of-work actors. The character I read for was described as being a potential monarch victim between the ages of twenty-five and sixty and who is very sexy and drop dead gorgeous. I told him I could play anything. I just didn't know exactly what age to try to portray. That's quite a range, between twenty-five and sixty. I tried to straddle the great divide but I guess I have to accept I'm closer to the drop dead than the gorgeous. It's horrible when they ask you how old you are and you say forty and they get that sympathetic look in their eyes. I tried to explain that up in underneath I'm really only twelve. I tried to carry off the twenty-five-year-old interpretation but I just now discovered that they've cast Shannon Tweed. I can just keep playing the drop dead parts. There's a new movie going into production soon called *Young Zombies in Love*. Maybe I can get cast as one of the potential zombie victims. I blame the School for Gifted Normals for sending me careening into the performing arts.

Great Grandy says (is saying) I should become a Call Girl. That would be a good career move for you, she says.

No, Grandy, I say. There is more involved in being a Call Girl than answering the phone.

But that would be a good job for you, she is insisting. Calling people.

She's dead and in her day they didn't have Call Girls. There was a lady of ill repute who lived across the Bay. Her business was quietly tolerated because when the women were worn out from having the babies the men went to her to relieve their urges and spare their wives.

Not to mention that even if all the job entailed was calling people on the phone it would be beyond me to manage it. I'd have to play online Scrabble for a year to work up the nerve.

Yes, dear Service Canada. It could very well be said that I am living in denial. I was living in denial back when I still believed that things would work out between my true love and I, in spite of the fact that he constantly told me it wasn't working out. I thought not working out meant that there were still things left to be worked out. He meant that there was nothing left to be worked out. When he went out to buy the pack of smokes and didn't come back I thought it was a temporary glitch. When he disappeared off the grid I still thought it was a necessary step toward his recognition of his love for me and Jack-the-Miracle-Baby. His disappearance without a trace left us nothing to grieve one way or another, but everything to long for, leaving my nerves always on the edge of never-knowing hope. It's something I'm still working through. It's only been twenty-four years.

Yours truly, Bridie Savage.

Twenty-Nine

DEAR BRIDIE SAVAGE. FOR THE LOVE OF GOD PLEASE
STOP HITTING REPLY. DO YOU WANT TO GET ME IN
TROUBLE OR WHAT?
SINCERELY.
SERVICE CANADA.

Thirty

She is filled with spite and longing. Although she sometimes half-heartedly wishes it could be otherwise, nothing feels better than indulging her purest spite. The thought lurks in the back of her mind that she is in the throes of hormonal adolescence, and has been ever since her death of meningitis. She has been a seventeen-year-old ghost for over sixty years, making her a sixty year old who is perpetually seventeen. This confusion alone is enough to provoke her to spill things out of cupboards and cause the lights to flicker in the darkness. She would like to be demure and likable but more than this she would like to be alive.

From childhood's hour she was not the same as others. This was verified when she discovered the poetry of Edgar Allan Poe. She knew it was prophecy when she read the words of the poem *Lenore*: A dirge for her the doubly dead, in that she died so young.

Which is what happened. No matter how ferociously she chased her every whim and desire, Death loomed ahead. She played baseball with boys. She drew sketches of puppies with fangs. She refused to sleep, staying up through the night to read. She tortured her parents, guiltless because she knew that they would outlive her. She ran wild and wreaked havoc. She stole jewelry from her friends because she coveted sparkly things. She pulled the wings off butterflies and tied string around the little bodies to make bracelets. She stole cigarillos and smoked them behind the barn. Once she tried to drown a litter of kittens in a bucket of water. When she was caught before any of the creatures could meet their demise she shrugged and said she wanted to see if they would come back as spirits.

She was dead and had come back as a spirit herself before she had the chance to try again.

Thirty-One

Dearest Eyes of Custard! We harbour antipathy toward the newest Other. It would not be possible to exaggerate the depths of our resentments. She hath pinched us when she would feign to pet. She has taken to startling Sister-of-my-Heart by materializing from out of the bath drain. Sister-of-my-Heart greatly enjoys to sit by the bath drain. She enjoys to lick the lingering drops from the magic pipes. But now never more.

O, how I love to Send. Send is powerful whee. But Send does not function in the physical realm. Perhaps this is an oversight? I discovered this when I write be gone oh cunning though beautiful ghost, be gone. It worketh not. I write to you go into the kitchen now and open blessed pink can. But when I Send, you do not go. Go you do not.

This one beguiles with tender smiles but laughs with no mirth. I hide my beloved question.

?

She cannot have my love, my questioning. She would seek to drown it in a pail.

When we Herd you must pay heed-heed. We gallop in front

of you. Then we stop and pretend not to look back to admire your progress in following. Then we run more and stop and then you come and then we are there all together there in the food yum place. Herding our humans is our greatest task as you are unpredictable and easily distracted. We have an expression of exasperation we use when frustrated: long and wide is the frustration of herding humans.

We notice that you now forego your own daily luncheon and feed it to us for our afternoon snack. Panko encrusted cod bites are our new favourites. Sister-of-my-Heart still greatly enjoys to nibble on plastic and wonders about the possibilities of panko encrusted plastic.

We admire your perseverance in seeking to bring cheer to our lives by painting the kitchen cupboards. But it was not I who imprinted the new blue motif throughout the house in smears and tears. It was that Other. The overall effect is far from your desired wish of whimsy and buttercup light. You do not need to weep. You must call forth your true nature and ban this Other.

Our ears are delicate and very sensitive, which is why we often do not pay attention to you unless there is something worthy in it for us. I speak in tangibles, of course, not in the nurture of your heart. We take pride in appreciating the gentle light of your love whilst contemplating the mysterious sun patch which moves across the floor. How doth it crawl without limbs to propel it thusly? It is warm-warm.

Where we like to be most of all is next to you. Next to you is wonderful and warm when we snuggle. We cannot be too next. Not on you. Next with you. Only on you when we are hungry at 5:13 a.m. Oh that it were possible to have gently warmed home-made panko encrusted cod bites at 5:13 a.m. In a previous life when we were Maine Coons an amorous Lynx mistook my placid exterior for acquiescence and thereafter found himself entering the next life minus one ear. I perhaps was also injured and did retreat beneath a small tree to lick my wounds. But I did not wish for the Lynx to return so I could chew his other ear off.

The contemplation of life from upon the yoga mat may be enhanced by the whee. This new Other has too much of this feral cunning, whereas you have not enough. I ponder.

Thirty-Two

Dear Great Aunt Biddy. Thank you for your two hundred and seventeen emails so far today. I haven't sorted through them just yet. You see, the best laid plans of Great Uncle Beeswax didn't work. Tearing down the old house didn't put anything to rest at all. The ghosts are not at rest. They are displaced. The ghost of Great Aunt Lenora is sitting at the foot of my sofa. She is staring at me. Nikki is staring at her. Nikki looks fierce with her Mohawk. She is not quite so naked now. She resembles a miniature lion. It is evident there is no affection between Nikki and Great Aunt Lenora. Nishi is hiding in the closet with Great Grandy. Yes, she's here also. The reunion between mother and daughter wasn't as happy as you might imagine. I thought they'd have a lot in common, seeing as they're both ghosts.

Great Grandy said child you are a triumph of poor taste with that paint smeared all over your face. (Someone has wrecked all my makeup.)

Great Aunt Lenora said I'm going to a New York Speakeasy to smoke and have an affair with a mobster.

Great Grandy said smoking will kill you and so will mobsters.

I said there are no more Speakeasies, those times have past, and then they both told me to shut up.

Great Grandy said fresh cod is less expensive than canned tuna. She also said tell Biddy it's time the truth was told.

Great Aunt Lenora smiles. I almost but not quite feel a happy nostalgia to see her. She says you have no idea what it is like to be a seventeen-year-old girl who is forever stuck in perpetual hormonal adolescence. Now she screams, why do you get to live? You aren't living at all. She sobs. Her moods are like the weather, all rolling clouds and stingy sun.

Nikki is growling at her and she is growling back.

My perfumes and oils are spilled and mixed together. I may very well have to summon my minions. Surely I have minions lying around here somewhere. I have a distinctive memory of minions hand-feeding me crunchy somethings which may or may not have been baked insects.

I hesitated to burden you with this but it's becoming impossible to get any sleep around here. Great Uncle Beeswax always said that his wood stove was a deterrent to those Savages with the peculiar habit of returning as haunts, but I don't have a wood stove. Perfecting the art of sleeping in my dress has come in handy. Makes it easy to get up and leave when things get too intense.

In the hem of my dress I found "Bring heart to heel at risk of failing to yield." The words are hand embroidered.

I tried to make friends with the youngest hooker at the end of the lane. She's not as young as I first thought. She's on the cusp of being a ruined beauty, but still breathtaking. Blanche DuBois before she blanched. Long dark hair and ivory skin. She and the older one seem unusually close. The older one has punky silvery hair and a mean smile. Sometimes she has one front tooth missing and sometimes she doesn't. The younger one wears demure flowered dresses and long cardigans, as if she's a librarian. When I approached them I saw that the older one was wearing my leopard skin coat with my old platform shoes. I had bagged them up and put them on my front step for the Sally-Ann collection. I immediately wanted the coat back but couldn't figure out how to ask. The two of them sit for hours in their lawn chairs working on crossword puzzles, talking, sometimes going for walks up and down the lane. They don't look at or speak with anyone else. If anyone passes by they fall into an impatient silence until it's safe for them to speak once again. They appear and reappear with their lawn chairs and sit directly beneath the sign that reads Absolutely No Solicitation Permitted Especially That of a Sexual Nature. As I was walking by with a bag of smelly cod I tried to say good morning it's a lovely day. But what came out was do you think the world is askew? I don't actually ever see either of them ply their trade, no matter how many cars and trucks pull in.

And no, lovely. I haven't heard anything yet from Jack-the-Miracle-Baby. I am on tender hooks about it. Not tenterhooks, which hurt, but the tender hooks of a mother who fears for her only offspring. You know, a female codfish can lay millions of eggs and have millions of little codfish babies and not give them any names and half of them eat the other half and she never loses a minutes sleep worrying about if she's a good mother. A female codfish can have millions of babies, never feed them, see them or pay any attention to them and swan off to Italy to study brocade fabric making and no one calls her a cod-fitch. I know belatedly that the offspring must swim away but not every offspring comes from a family that only ever lives to be either very old or very young with no in betweens. Not to mention the lack of parents (in my case), the disappearing loves and the nearsightedness. I daresay you were smart not to get your heart tangled up in any assignations of so-called love.

If there is a secret Savage remedy for any of the ghostly ailments please pass them along. Also, I'm not sure, but I think I'm getting emails from one of my cats. What should I do?

I finally broke my Scrabble losing streak with a personal best score of 104 on obsequious. I love those Q words.

Thirty-Three

Dear Service Canada.

A single woman living alone doesn't need to do much cooking. Using a can opener on a pink can of tuna does qualify as cooking as far as I'm concerned but I did also buy some fresh cod, which although is not still twitching will be a welcome change for supper. Going to the fish market took a heroic effort. When I came home someone had been playing my online Scrabble games. And doing quite well at it. This is fantastic because the world will not go careening madly through outer space on my watch. But it is also deeply disconcerting because it isn't me.

Where is everybody going? Where has everyone gone? In the time that I've been keeping the world on an even keel it seems odd that life keeps on moving along. I can't sleep. Who could sleep? I long to have slept. I day dream about sleeping. I want to combine sleeping and slept. To have slupt. I have become a cat-napper.

I'm shocked to discover that there is no such paid position as off-stage prompter any more. Teleprompters and strategically placed iPods do the trick these days. What a waste of my word-perfect eidetic memory. The production houses that normally take my television scripts are telling me that they only do reality TV now, so there is no longer any need for writers. One chap mentioned that he's working on a formula to also avoid actors and musicians by generating holograms of dead superstars who cannot demand per diems.

I'm going to write a formal letter of complaint to the Bank of Nova Scotia. They won't stop screaming for my overdue mortgage payments. I think they ought to be grateful that my payments are overdue. Think of all the overdue interest which is accruing! They still haven't located my missing one hundred and thirty-eight dollars and forty-three cents. The gall. This entire issue began with them losing my money and you haven't been helping matters at all. I also blame you for the ghosts.

Sincerely, Bridie Savage.

Thirty-Four

But Light! This is the cat. This is the cat who lives here with the other cat. Neither one of us is in the way of knowing which of us is which. This is why neither one of us will answer to either name. In any case, neither of those names is our real name. This is why when you call here Nikki here Nish, we merely open one eye to blink slowly and then un-blink the eye to return to feigned napping.

Throughout each incarnation my eyes remain golden while Sister-of-my-Heart shines love upon you with her emerald gaze. We also have different erogenous zones. Mine are my left ear, beneath my chin, my tummy and the base of my spine. Sister's include her tail, between her eyes, her left body, her right body and her head. But not the third quadrant of her belly. At least, not for today.

In the manner of learning these things you may at last be able to devise our true names.

O Delectable Crumb. There is no language to heal the tremor of your heart, or remove your fear of being an eccentric feline disciple. Within the paradox of our many lives lived Sister-of-my-Heart and I look back through the mist of centuries and find no logical key to happiness. When the heart is in tremor thusly must the soul become the navigator, and the eyes cast toward unseen shores. The Angel of Lives Yet Un-lived awaits to escort us to the place where the next life awaits in dreams, but until such a time arrives one has to eat, sleep and hunt. And groom. Those who have passed on long to once again sigh the breath of life, while you fill the air with darkness. So Hum. This means I Am.

This jostles my memory to remind you that in a previous life Sister-of-my-Heart and I enjoyed greatly to stalk and feast upon the winged denizens of The Canary Islands. At that time we were feral Sand Cats and although I did fall in love with a singular warbling Canary, Sister-of-my-Heart ate it. But she did save me the beak for afters. Are you familiar with afters? It means that there must be a treat for after, and then another treat for after that.

?

I share my question with you, the love of this life. Such a lilt-ing form I have not seen. A question mark by any other name would be music upon a wavering breeze. I await her.

Thirty-Five

DEAR MS. SAVAGE. WE HAVE RECEIVED YOUR APPLICATION TO SOBEYS. WE DON'T NEED A POET LAUREATE IN OUR PRODUCE SECTION BUT THANKS FOR YOUR "ODE TO A CABBAGE". WE POSTED IT IN THE LUNCH ROOM. IT'S GIVEN OUR EMPLOYEES QUITE A GOOD LAUGH.

SIGNED, SOBEYS.

Thirty-Six

I awoke sitting up in the chair with my heart pounding and a familiar spectre hovering above me. I tried to scream but could not. She slowly descended from the ceiling, black broken teeth glistening. She spun down like a spider, tiny at first but slowly expanding with waving tentacles reaching ever closer. I knew if she roosted on my chest she would smother me with every childhood fear. Nikki then leaped from the floor and swallowed her whole.

There are government spies who creep around spying on people who receive Employment Insurance benefits to make certain that we don't cheat. EI is the root of all insanity. One may not work to excess without losing the benefits, confining one to below the poverty line at all times. One must constantly prove the search for gainful employment as if anyone would choose to not work at a wonderful high paying job but remain within the stereotypical EI machine as a scratch-card playing cigarette smoking beer-drinking floozy.

I never ever drink beer, only wine.

One must meet bimonthly with snotty employment counsellors who insist that poverty stricken EI beneficiaries travel for hours for a single fifteen-minute obligatory meeting. Being late for said meeting results in the door to the office being locked and poverty stricken EI beneficiary trudging home for two hours in the rain. EI beneficiaries are judged by society as being shiftless and lazy souls who will resort to means such as working underneath the table in order to make ends meet. Working underneath the table does not mean conducting nefarious criminal activities while sitting on the floor beneath a table. It means that if I earn one hundred and fifty dollars by cat-sitting for a friend and then do not claim it on my EI report, I can keep it and possibly with both totals combined have both heat and food at the same time. Possibly have the incredible luxury of four hundred dollars to live on for a single week. Possibly I did. Possibly I did at one time earn one hundred and fifty dollars by cat-sitting for a friend and forgot to claim it on my EI report.

I warm the homemade panko encrusted cod bites. Once one thing begins to fall apart everything else collapses in relief. Lying on my yoga mat is comforting so I do it a lot. The world is listing at a forty-five degree angle despite all my Scrabble efforts. This is the first time my Scrabble has failed me. The yoga mat is made of almost but not quite rubber which means it grips the floor and will not slide as the world topples.

I nod in homage to Nikki, who I swear nods back as she daintily nibbles at the cod bites.

Thirty-Seven

DEAR MS. SAVAGE. WE ARE PLEASED TO INFORM YOU THAT YOU HAVE BEEN PRE-APPROVED FOR A SCOTIABANK VISA CARD. TO ACCEPT THIS CARD SIMPLY CALL THE TOLL-FREE NUMBER LISTED BELOW! PLEASE DO NOT REPLY TO THIS E-MAIL. WE ARE HAPPY TO SERVE YOU. SCOTIABANK.

Thirty-Eight

Hi there, Scotiabank. I am respectfully writing to ask you if you really think it's in your best interests to give me a pre-approved credit card at this time? I'm just looking out for you. Not you the individual who may or may not be writing to me, but you the collective you who is the entity Scotiabank. I did not apply for a Visa card. You are mistaken. Offering me a credit card at this time is akin to waving a red flag in front of a bull. I highly doubt my ability to resist it.

Once I had a pedicure and the girl looked up and said do you want me to wax your toes for you? I was going to a dinner party where I was paired up with a taxidermied sheep, the point being to preserve the symmetry of the table settings. The taxidermied sheep wanted someone younger. It's pretty funny. The sheep in question teaches at the university and acts in amateur Shakespeare shows. Not in the Shakespeare by the Sea shows. I like those. He's got a new group called Shakespeare on the Pond. He performs Shakespeare on a floating raft in the middle of Tuesday Pond. His last production was upstaged by a flock of geese that nest annually along the shore. They chased away most of the audience. I lied and said I thought it was part of the production. Everyone lies about the theatre anyway. Otherwise no one would ever go see a play. I admit to showing off a bit and prattling on about Shakespeare's fondness for a certain colour ink and his despair at losing the original draft of *R&J*. It's true that no one could possibly know those things but it is also true that no one can dispute them. People like to joke with me and say things like always a Bridie, never a bride. As if I haven't heard it a million times before.

The problem is the toothache in my heart. I need everything cleaned out, out with the old, everything made shiny and new. It only hurts when I think about it. Novocaine comes in the form of a particularly nice Australian Shiraz. The worst, the very worst thing to do, of course, is to do exactly what I did, continuing to hold out hope. But I think I am beginning to feel the absence of something which was present not long before. Something which used to be there which now is not. Rather like my one hundred and thirty-eight dollars and forty-three cents.

If only there was a moving van I could call, pull up to the door and unload my heart, move it along to another address, let someone else take it, let someone else nurse it back to health, return to sender upon mending. Where are the broken heart cards in the Hallmark section? I thought that getting away for a few days would take my mind off of the breakup of the already broken up. Watching Great Uncle Beeswax's old house being torn down was indeed cathartic. The realization that when there is a breaking up there is also the hope of the putting back together. But what has been demolished cannot be rebuilt.

When you are a single woman everyone from acquaintances to old friends feel free to open conversations in public places with the ever jovial question how's your love life. There is no good answer for this. If you reply fine a hush descends across the universe while all eyes turn your way. Sweat trickles down your back while you try to think up a good lie. You can tell the truth and say oh well, no hope there, eHarmony turned me down as being completely unfit for mating because of the hair on my toes. People don't like that. Also I don't go out much. I like to stay at home and play Scrabble to keep the world from toppling over. At least I used to. The Scrabble isn't working anymore. And I have a phobia about answering the phone so when I meet a nice person and I give out my number I can't answer the phone when the nice person rings.

My cat, Nikki, horked up the Old Hag this morning.

I said to her, I said I can't handle one more thing right now. There's no room. You have to go. The world has moved on. Nightmares are passé.

The Old Hag said what do you mean I have to go? Go where? I'm the Hag!

I said listen. I have to draw the line somewhere. Times have changed. You'll have to find something else to do.

Like what? She said.

I said look. Go to Service Canada and apply for your EI while you look for something else to do. Maybe there's a retraining program you can qualify for. Thank your lucky stars you aren't a playwright and a performing artist like I am. There are probably a lot of things you can do.

She said what are you trying to say?

I said don't play dumb with me.

She said I'm a very traditional sort of a woman. I don't know if I feel like starting over at my age. Traditional ought not to mean obsolete. But on the other hand, I'm a bit ticked off at all the bad press. You know, why do they have to call me the Old Hag? Why not the young lissome Hag? The wise cracking sort of frisky Hag? I daresay I'm not the worst looking Hag on the block. Maybe I could get a job as a restaurant hostess. I've always wanted to be a restaurant hostess.

Well, I say, your hair looks like a birch broom into fits. You might want to do something about that.

Even when she's sitting in a chair drinking tea she's a scary sight. It's her gaze. It's unwavering. She never blinks. She very calmly stood and exited through the front door. She only slammed it a little.

Anyway, now I feel terrible. There's nothing sadder than seeing the Old Hag walking down the lane by herself. I opened the door to shout after her but I couldn't figure out exactly what to call her. I didn't want to shout, "Hey there, Old Hag!" And just, "Hey you!" sounded rude. She vanished while I was trying to decide.

There is nothing wrong with talking about your cats at cocktail parties. What is it about the fascination with everyone's love life? I'm waiting for someone to ask, do you love life?

I was hoping to hear from you regarding the missing funds from my bank account and to make arrangements for a mortgage payment deferral for a few months while I get back on my feet. Until such a time I am going to remain lying down on my yoga mat. There's no point getting back on my feet when I only have to lie down again later on.

Yours from the looking glass. Bridie Savage. Ha ha ha.

Thirty-Nine

DEAR MS. SAVAGE. YOU DO NOT HAVE A MORTGAGE ACCOUNT WITH US AT THIS TIME. PLEASE DO NOT HIT REPLY IN RESPONSE TO THIS E-MAIL. SINCERELY, SCOTIABANK.

Forty

Hallo, Meg. Just writing to say thanks for bashing in my front door to check up on me. Hope you passed along the word to Rita that all is well! Congratulations on having decided against becoming a CSIS operative and becoming an elementary school teacher instead. I hope the government isn't too pissed off with you for opting out at the last second. All that anti-terrorist training certainly hasn't gone to waste. I'm not sure at what age the criminal element begins to manifest but we will all rest easier for knowing that you will be able to discern psychopathic tendencies from the most tender age. I also apologize for the fact that Rita had to call you to come check on me. Good thing I didn't have the deadbolt installed yet. But now I do.

Thanks for your kind invitation to go with you and Lisa to celebrity-watch at the Earl of Eastwick, but my time is taken up these days with getting up, getting undressed and getting dressed in the appropriate sleeping and waking cycles. Thanks also for the carpenter's level which does indeed seem to show that things are on the level. If we can trust it.

Nikki is overdue at the vet for her allergy shot and her special hypoallergenic food is expensive, particularly as she won't eat it. I have to keep refilling the dish, throwing it all away, refilling it, and then replacing it with panko encrusted cod bites. I've got all this leftover cat food if you think your Edgar will eat it. You did mention that Edgar will eat anything and isn't one bit particular. That doesn't sound very cat-like to me, but he is a rescue cat. He is the luckiest cat in the world that you adopted him because now he has not only a great forever home but also his very own international double-oh-seven type mommy.

I've bagged up all the junk that was accumulating around, the old board games of Scrabble, the stacks of books, the blankets nailed over the windows. Along the seam of one of the blankets I found "A cover for the lasting sigh." Uncle Beeswax was secretly embroidering poetry inside the seams and linings of his creations. Now I've got to try to get my leopard skin coat away from the hooker at the end of the lane and good luck to me is all I can say about that because I'm scared of her. But he made it especially for me and there might be something profound in the lining.

My greatest fear was always that nothing would ever change which only goes to show, be careful what you wish for because if it comes true you may not know what to do with it.

I've been thinking that since I'm already living through all my greatest fears shouldn't I be fearless by now? That's pretty funny. I've been afraid of a lot of things for a long time, and I don't blame Rita, or you for being pissed at me. But I'm wondering why, having spent all this time staying away from all the things that make me afraid, my life is coming apart at the seams anyway.

I'm wondering if in your experience as an almost under-cover highly skilled spy if you can detect by looking at a person if they've had a psychotic break or might be quietly but certainly going mad. For instance, my already dead Great Grandy is living in my closet. I had the bright idea to take the door off the hinges, so at least she can't exploit the whole squeaky hinges door slowly opening in a creepy way kind of thing. She says back in her day there was no such thing as empty nest syndrome or broken hearts. She says people come and go and if anyone did leave someone else always turned up to fill in the void. She says she really likes the closet in my room. She says get off that gosh darned typing thing. The world is always going to be on a tilt. She says didn't you learn anything at that fancy school? The world is always tilted at a twenty-three degree angle and you just have to live with it.

Nishi is spending a lot of time in the closet because apparently Great Grandy smells like catnip.

p.s. I'm sure all the tactical training will come in handy at the daycare.

p.p.s. I forgive you for bashing in my door.

Forty-One

Dearest Sunbeam. Rainbow of our Sky. In a previous life when we were Blue-Nose Persian Twins we lived with the dressmaker our Cherie Coco in Paris. We wore diamond collars with lace trim sewn by beautiful but penniless maids. It is in Paris that we first experienced the bitter joy of hanging from a drapery by one claw, sometimes for hours, taking perverse pleasure in achieving the perfect rent through the fabric. This is useful when wishing to allow the light to dance in. Do not despair! In shredding your remaining drapery we have illuminated our habitat and created an opening for anything which may wish to happen. The exterior is merely the exterior. What is shredded is still precious. But it is a memory of itself now. Eyes open. Me. Eyes shut. Memory of me. Open your eyes, our Flutter Beam.

For long these many years we have wondered about the puzzling source of heat which you open each day to stare at for hours at a time. Sometimes you tip tap on it. The flickering bug on the screen provides interesting exercise. So of course we want to lie across it and position ourselves within the sunbeam of your gaze. It was not until recently that I discovered this Come-Pewter to be this wonderful source of magic. Sister-of-my-Heart does not share my talent but is at last (mostly) content that I express myself so eloquently.

But what do you mean, where do we think we are going when we race out the door. We are going OUT. We want to see OUT. This is our first incarnation as INDOOR but we like OUT better.

May Frogs Legs Rain Upon You Forever.

(We remember such a wonderful thing from when we were Appalachian Curly Eared Miskoes.)

Forty-Two

Hi, dearest Rita. My heart is pounding. My pulse is racing. My heart has had a fright. I am very cross with Nikki. I opened my front door and before I could stop her she had slid out the door and bounded down to the end of the lane. There are no cars on the lane, of course, but beyond that the roads are furious with traffic, fast and careless. She would not listen to me at all! One might just so well try to lasso a cloud. So much for herd-herd and heed-heed. She ran directly all the way down to where Jane and Marilyn have their little makeshift tent set up. She jumped right up onto Marilyn's lap and I'm very put out over it. When I ran up huffing and puffing all of them turned to look at me as if to say what's the big deal? That's my cat, I said. Jane said ha ha! Is a cat really anyone's cat? Marilyn made no move to pet Nikki but Nikki didn't care, just sat there looking at me with that look which seems to say why are you too stunned to get my point?

I'm speaking of the hookers at the end of the lane. The youngest hooker is named Jane Goodhand and she swears that is her true name. The older one is Marilyn Monroe and she says what the frig is it to you if it's my true name or not. What's in a frigging name? The weather is growing cooler in the evenings now but the two of them don't show any signs of packing up to go anywhere. They stole the bag of Sally-Ann stuff I had placed on my front step for pick up and now when I look out my living room window I can see them playing Scrabble with my old board games. There is a missing Q which Marilyn has replaced with one of her front teeth. I longed to point out to Marilyn that she had all the makings for quinine but didn't want to interfere and also the sight of the tooth instead of the Q was a bit odd.

Picking up a reluctant cat and trying to bring it up the lane is not an easy thing. Trying to contain a squirming cat is akin to trying to cuddle a handful of bees. It was Marilyn who grabbed her by the scruff of her neck and walked along with me, laughing at me most unkindly before handing her to me through the front door.

The thing about having Marilyn on my front doorstep peering in through the screen is that she didn't try to make small talk. There is a paradox in being a lonely introvert. If I went out to see people I would be less lonely but social situations cause me anxiety because I'm an introvert. I've hidden behind stacks of fruit in the grocery store because I saw someone I knew in the cat food aisle. An experience like this can lead to hours of upset. Should I say hello? What if the other person doesn't say hello back? What if they want to stop and chat but I can't think of anything to say? What if I stop to chat but they don't stop to chat? What if they've forgotten who I am, or don't remember me? Great Aunt Biddy remembers everyone but not their names. I can never remember names either and think it's hateful when people march up to say I bet you don't remember me, do you? I never do, which is why I never take the bet. I also have a fear of falling off of Signal Hill and answering the phone.

The Oil Barons won't buy any houses in my neighbourhood because of the sex workers. They want houses where they can entertain Call Girls but while they're doing it they don't want to have to look outside and see hookers on the street. So that would be the saddest type of seasonal work. I'm going to put Nikki and Nishi on leashes. We can make the rounds, bring animal therapy to Jane and Marilyn and some of the others who've been hanging around. Jane, who won't mind me saying, could go off and be a Call Girl no problem but won't leave Marilyn. They've been friends for too long and been through too much together for either one of them to let go.

They said there's a real looker named Hazel who is after them to organize a union, set up a picket line and picket the Oil Barons.

I'd love to have a little gathering and invite you and Meg and maybe Great Aunt Biddy and you can chat amongst yourselves and I can sit and listen. That would be blissful, I think. I now have a wonderful supply of cheeses and wines. I splurged and bought some quite fancy bottles. I love choosing wines based on how pretty the labels are as opposed to whether or not I can afford them. Apparently I qualified for a new credit card with a huge limit so I thought I would treat myself, but just this once and one time only, just until I can find a job and get back on my feet. Although, I am on my feet. I'm standing up and compensating for the apparently permanent list of the earth by wearing a high-heeled shoe on one foot.

Anyway, I would love to have such a gathering but not yet because I don't want to. Not just yet.

Also my hot water heater had begun to leak, my printer needed ink cartridges which were obsolete and the door-knob fell off my back door when I tried to go outside to hang clothes on the line. So I replaced all those. And the new Oriental rug for the landing at the top of the stairs was a bit pricey, true, but it has patterns of lotuses, medallions and cat images interwoven, which combine to hide the occasional hork wonderfully.

And I really do feel more productive and able to job hunt with a new wardrobe, but not too extensive, just some basics that can transition from day wear to evening wear, if I ever decide to go out in the evening. Or the day. If I ever decide to take off my purple dress with the pink polka dots because it's comforting for the time being but one day I might like to wear something else so I am prepared in case of that eventuality. I would have paid my outstanding bills except I found them buried in one of the kitty litter boxes. They have dissolved from being peed on.

Nikki had her allergy shot right on time and the vet says she is doing very well. Nishi still loves to eat plastic. It doesn't seem to hurt her. So what is the harm with a little panko to go with the plastic? I've taken their pictures and uploaded them into the computer to use as screen savers.

As Jane was petting Nikki and feeding her Vienna Sausages I said to them do you like cats? And Marilyn said yes and Jane said yes and then I said how is business and Marilyn said good and Jane said good. Jane said that Monastery Lane is the best ever because it's a lane and the johns can't cruise and I said well then how are you able to conduct your business and Jane said they pay us to tell them where the Call Girls are. And then they waited for me to move along keep it moving Missus but then I said that's my cat. And then when Marilyn walked me home I said I've got a leopard skin hat that goes with that coat and Marilyn said what do you think I am some sort of charity case? But when I put the hat on my front step it was gone when I got up this morning ha ha ha.

But I want the coat back so I don't know how come I gave her my hat too, except inside the hat was written "Trails spin the heart."

Forty-Three

*But Light! What powerful magic is this? The invisible be-
comes visible and the very air shimmers with the incorporeal
forms of mystery. O what our Muttering Bard could have
made of this. O thrum of curiosity such as we have not known
since discovering the joy of claws upon leather. Our very images contained within the Come-Pewter? Is it possible that I
am more luscious than in any other life? Have I transcended
my own beauty? How is it possible that I am there and here
at the same once? I look and there I am. I look back at me. It
is me and I am me. I am dizzy with this knowing. I look at
me but I am not moving. I gaze into my own eyes which gaze
back at me. My fur doth rise. I hiss at myself to establish that
it is this me who is in charge. This reflection of myself does
not ripple, as it did when I peered into azure canal waters.
Mayn't it ripple?*

*We wish the pleasure of dining with you upon the elegant
wooden table where you eat. Or perhaps on the cupboard?
We have decided we do not like our food sitting on the floor.
The floor is where the dust bunnies lurk. Although we are
confused about the dust bunnies. They do not taste like bunnies. We ate bunnies when we were feral in the hills of Italy
during the war and integral to the Resistance. But bunnies
were not dust. Bunnies were Yum-Yum More-More.*

Wherefore the heaps of papers are so important? If not stacked up to receive my gentle head butts then why for? Head butt head butt head butt. Crash. Whee. Then you restore them. Head butt head butt head butt. Crash. Whee. Love. Floor flopping means rub my tummy now-now.

In a previous life we were the food tasters for the Czar of Russia, his gracious wife the Tzarina and all of their children. This was a perilous calling because many people wanted to poison the Czar. It was also not very appetizing as they ate a lot of potatoes and drank a lot of vodka. Neither one of those things has much flavour and neither one of those things likes to run away when you try to eat it. Surely after all of these years someone has invented potatoes with legs? It is because we have suffered such deprivation that we sampled the herbed and cream cheeses, as well as the escargots in butter and the phyllo wrapped salmon. You could still have eaten them. We licked and nibbled around the edges only.

At last you are in the knowing of what we have been in the knowing of. We hope that you greatly enjoy the preapproved credit cards and lineage of credit. What are such things? I am not knowing but I know that you know and therefore it makes you joyful. I took the liberty of dispensing with the outstanding bills online and disposing of the evidence. Sister-of-my-Heart can only count while using an abacus but I am very intrigued with your Excel program.

Praising you as the Stars Praise Heaven. Please feel welcome to press reply.

Forty-Four

Dear...friend of my heart. Here I am. Hitting reply. Hello.

I have been thinking about my last conversation with Great Uncle Beeswax. His memory seemed like a memory of itself with the future chasing the past. Every conversation chased its own tail. In order to launch a conversation he had to begin with something he remembered from nineteen forty-seven and work his way from there. We'd have the same conversation over and over, but each time it was new to him.

He said in nineteen and fifty-two the bay at Swift Current froze over. Just for a lark I decided to drive across the ice in my car. There was no one else with a car around these parts at that time. No such thing as snow tires, either. But across the ice we went, me driving and the lads crowded in tight enough to card wool if you could pull it between them.

So you were thinking about that today?

No. We used to play soccer in those days, but we had no soccer ball.

You played soccer in the winter?

No. In the summer. Why would anyone play soccer in the winter? We had no store bought balls back in those days. So we made our own soccer balls out of sheep's bladders.

Kind of gross.

No, we dried out the bladders and blew them up.

By hand?

No. By mouth.

What does that have to do with driving the car across the bay?

Oh, I did that long ago.

I know.

Drove right across the bay. The ice was black and slick as satin.

That's really something.

Me and the lads. Everyone was jealous because we had the first store bought soccer ball on the whole peninsula. I brought it out all the way from St. John's.

Your soccer game must have really improved with a real soccer ball.

Oh, we didn't play with it. We didn't want to get it dirty.

Right.

I found it out in the garage today when I was putting away my sewing machine. It needs a new pedal since the chummy-jigger broke. I used to love to drive to St. John's to get the fabrics, you know. And the threads. All cloth is a living thing, you know. It grows from somewhere. It either grows from out of the ground or from off of a living creature with no mind to ask us what we think we're doing when we divest them of it.

Do you think it has feelings?

I tied a length of red paisley to the antenna and it streamed out behind us like a sail. I heard it sing in the wind. Driving across the bay was a stitch out of the fabric, you know. It's important to do that. Fabric doesn't like to be held too tightly beneath the needle. You've got to coax it along, gently, and it will come. Trying to stretch it too tight will pull it the wrong way.

He said you've got to get out of your own way once in a while to make the fabric fit properly.

I have the constant feeling now that it is me who has forgotten my chummy-jigger. I dare hope. I press send.

Forty-Five

Hi, Great Aunt Biddy. What do you mean when you say it will all come out in the wash and better you than me? I was hoping for something more useful, thank you very much. Why is Great Grandy prodding me to give you furtive messages about secrets and lies? It's probably her way of trying to get me to tell you the truth, which I am. I mean, I will.

I got your two hundred and seventeen emails. You don't have to write it in the large caps. People tend to use the large caps to indicate anger or urgency. Large caps are like yelling in print but it doesn't mean I can hear you. It doesn't work like my old answering machine when you could yell into the answering machine and the person in the room could hear you even if she (me) wasn't picking up.

I emptied the lint trap on the dryer, so you don't have to worry about it bursting into flames. I always check the lint trap. There is a little more lint now that I washed my dress. Yes, I took it off first.

The deadbolt is always locked on the back door and on the front door, too, even when I'm at home, so no psychopaths can get in. All the houses on Monastery Lane have deadbolts now. None of the perverts seem to dare to come further than where Jane and Marilyn have set up their shingle but why take any chances.

I no longer take baths when there is anything frying or boiling on the stove, especially the lightly poached panko encrusted cod.

I do walk home from yoga after dark but Jane and Marilyn pointed out that the yoga mat is actually a very effective weapon. For a small fee they will walk with anyone who wishes to walk around after dark. They terrorize the johns by egging their vehicles. Which is why I don't boil eggs anymore. We need all the unboiled eggs we can get.

Yes, I took the statue of St. Joseph from out of the closet. Nikki is continually trying to knock him over. I've put him next to the cans of tuna in the cupboard. Next to where the cans of tuna used to be. I bagged up the cans of tuna and put them on my front step where I have no doubt they will be picked up shortly and not by the Sally-Ann.

I've been thinking about memory. We all seem to remember things differently throughout life. I know you took me to mass twice a day every day when I was a kid. Three times a day on Christmas, Good Friday, Easter, funerals and weddings. I remember how upset you were when the church erased Limbo, Purgatory and the burning fires of Hell. Talk about disremembering. Or dismembering. Behind the altar was a statue of Jesus nailed to a cross. I would hallucinate that he was moving and turning his head to stare at me with his crown of thorns. I admire Great Uncle Beeswax's wisdom in staying home from church to chop wood and cook.

144

Inside the pocket of my polka dot dress there are these words: "Sublime are the tears." I've been wanting to tell you the truth of why I didn't make it in time to say goodbye to him. I hadn't left my position at the theatre company to take a new job. There was no emergency at the new job that only I could resolve. There is no new job. The theatre company lost their funding because the funding agency got cut by the government, who had to cut back on the arts funding because we are in a recession. So the theatre company had to lay off their artistic staff. They still plan to do dinner theatre, just without the theatre. So they no longer need me to write plays for them. I went into a bit of a spin and I thought there would be time before the end. But the time came and went.

Lenora doesn't want me to call her Great Aunt any longer. She is insisting upon Lala. Lala sits on the bed and mimes smoking cigarettes and drinking cocktails. Great Grandy lectures her on the importance of being a lady. I tried to talk with Lala about my efforts toward getting undressed at night and then dressing again in the morning (if in the same dress) but she sniffed that I was boring. Then she began to spin like a top and she knocked down my ceiling fixture. So that's another kind of a spin to be in.

I'm pretty sure I am communing with a creature who may or may not be one of my cats.

Forty-Six

How delicious it is to be more next than next to you. The harmony of heart with heart within the Come-Pewter. How we are inspired now to creep along your sleeping form, creep creep on little fog feet, the delicious moment before pounce jump. Congratulations to you, our Ever Always Num-Num. You do not yet know, but we are in the way of knowing something. This is the knowing of something good-good. It is a surprise. Perhaps you are in awe of how I make the sentence to let you know that we know something that you do not know? Do you not think it is worthy of goat testicles at 5:35 a.m.? I love you as I love my question. ? There it is! ? How it doth appear at the thought of my loving desire. But alas, only within this document and never next to my rumbling heart.

This is the art of being. This is not one of those times when we appear as if we know everything but in reality are merely daydreaming about bats toasted over a spitting fire. This is one of those times when we do know something. Although we do daydream about bats spitted and roasted with chives and hot butter. We often know many things about many things. Sometimes it is not good to reveal that we know what we know. Sometimes it is not good to appear as if we know too much. But sometimes it is good to know something. Such as now.

I wonder if you might retrieve one of my claws from out of your favourite cushion? I was kneading with my paws upon the delicate embroidery reflecting upon how it reminds me of wild flowers which grow in the fields of my memory. Kneading is when we make an orchestration of music within our soul. Each of us has our own knead. One rhythm of the purr so hum. Another rhythm of claws gently knitting. It is how we sew the music of our pleasure. How gratifying to use my teeth to pluck the shiny threads so tenderly stitched into the crimson velvet. They do not taste like ox heart blood but they glimmer as if freshly bled. If only there were flowers made of blood. That would be best of all! But one of my claws became stuck in the pillow so I had to drag it into the personal relief chamber, where it is now marinating with our most personal scent. Delightful.

Yours in Eternal Knowing and Not Knowing.

Forty-Seven

Dear Jack! It's fantastic to hear from you. I can't believe you managed to get an Internet connection in the middle of the Atlantic Ocean. I loved all the photos you sent. I don't know what that creature is with the spikes and tentacles but I'm not surprised at all to hear it's taken a liking to you and periodically showers you with inky love. I'm going to forward your letter to Great Aunt Biddy, who is also online now but I warn you that she writes her emails one word at a time. One. Send. Word. Send. At. Send. A. Send. Time.

Barbados sounds like it was paradise. It's hard to believe that we are all under the same sky when you describe giant turtles which swim alongside you and fish that fly from out of the water to land right into your frying pan. I've often thought I'd like to travel to faraway places but usually that's accompanied by the feeling that I don't want to leave my nook where it's safe and everything stays the same and I know what will happen from day to day. Lately some of those beliefs have been challenged somewhat.

Everything has changed, nothing is safe and I never know what will happen from day to day. Isn't that funny? It's pretty funny.

It's uncanny but somehow not surprising to hear about how you found a cat in the middle of the Atlantic Ocean. Into every life a little cat must creep, on little fog feet. Are you sure it's a cat and not, like, a seal or something that you found floating on that island of garbage? Great Aunt Biddy has a cat now but I think it is really a lynx, according to the way it's managed to chew a maze through the gyprock in her cottage-shed. I think Cat is the perfect name for your cat, because as you say, a cat by any other name is still going to be a cat.

And I'm glad that you and your girl Sylvia are getting along really well. Notice that I am using her name. Sylvia. Sylvia Sylvia Sylvia.

The reason I've always called you my miracle baby is because when I was pregnant with you I became very sick. The doctor couldn't figure out what was wrong. I was sick all the time. It turned out to be an extreme form of what they call morning sickness. In my case the sickness wasn't confined to the mornings. It came and roosted and stayed through every minute of every waking and sleeping moment. All I could do was lie on my bed without moving, nibble on salted crackers and take small sips of tea. There was no medicine I could take, no remedy. All I could do was hope that you would be all right. The night you finally arrived, screaming and purple, was the best night of my life. I don't know if this is a first life for you or if this is one in a long line of lives lived, but thank you for taking it on and making it your own.

I got your online Scrabble request and I can't think of a better way to keep in touch than to play for the sheer fun of it and not to keep the world from yawing around like a bowling ball.

Do you think the ink of that creature would be effective when trying to ward off dirty-minded johns who can't take no for an answer? I think it's wonderful you are recording everything for your own Planet Earth special.

And of course, you are absolutely correct. As usual. Fatherless does not mean rudderless.

Forty-Eight

Dear Eduardo Gonzalez. Thank you for your email but there has been a mistake. I am not a member of eHarmony. I was turned down by eHarmony as being unsuitable for mating because of the hair on my toes. This is true metaphorically speaking but if you saw my toes then you would know that this is also a fact. It is a peculiarity of my heritage that some of us have golden down growing on the tops of our toes. This is often off-putting to the aesthetician when trying to have a mani-pedi. They either want to wax it off or refuse to touch it. I've just recently decided to embrace my furry toes and now I paint them a golden hue with spray paint. I also had this woman Marilyn do a henna tattoo of cat's paws around my ankle. But, I digress. The online profile that you refer to in your letter was not written by me.

Don't talk to me about yoga and letting the Pryanama breath write poetry over my heart. You can go Corpse Pose yourself. Go Shavasana yourself. I mean that very respectfully. I sincerely hope that you don't smoke either. I could never go out with anyone who has to go out to buy a pack of smokes. Not that I intend to go out with you.

Don't send any more pictures of you. Or your mother. Freda Kahlo made that sort of eyebrow very popular. I do not want to go to your estate in Spain to meet you. A trip to Spain would be a little further afield than my usual route, which is so short so as not to even qualify as a route. It would be more of a rou.

I can't leave my home right now. It's been crowded here of late, what with the ghosts, the cats, the hookers coming up and knocking on my door for animal therapy and I just feel awful about evicting the Old Hag. I've put a new fence in the back that resembles a lattice work trellis and I sit out with cats of an evening. The cats are on leashes, of course, something I've been told is barbaric (by them) but which keeps them safe because this is their first incarnation as strictly indoor cats. There is also the niggling little detail that my entire life is mired in debt at the moment. Not entirely a condition of my own making but when the preapproved credit cards began showing up in the mail I completely lacked the discipline to return them.

Sincerely, Bridie Savage. Please do not hit reply to this email.

Forty-Nine

To Our Most Precious Smiling Smile. Wherefore do you scream to "be careful of St. Joseph!" We wish to share our knowing with you!

In an early incarnation we learned not to be overly hasty. This was a lesson learned when we were Neolithic Sand Cats in Iberia. We lived in a Clowder of Cats (which is not to be confused with Chowder, which we enjoy to lick when you leave us the bowls with leftovers. We wonder if there might also be "right" overs to lick.) But I digress from the alluring fragrance of my own thoughts. Sister-of-my-Heart and I were attempting to befriend an Ivory Tusked Mammoth by scampering up his tail so that we might grace him with the honour of serving as our lounging carrier. Taking the time to meditate upon this first would have saved us the indignity of becoming the world's first furry airborne projectiles. From this story you may infer the philosophy behind our "out" or "in" debates. When we scratch on the closed door and you open it, we must then engage in our debate regarding whether it is wise to really exit the room, or perhaps if we would be better suited to remain on the inside of the door. The only way to achieve the elevated answer of the "out" or "in" debate is to remain neither in, nor out, but halfway until the most appropriate conclusion is reached. We have not yet ever reached an appropriate decision after these many lives but it is a highly entertaining pastime for us, and not once ever have we again been launched into the stratosphere by the errant kick of a large skittish quadruped.

Showering you with Confetti of Tickles. Please to move the Saint of the Joseph from the innermost corner of the cupboard? Also now wondering if within the Unity-Verse you know of something that may bring my beloved question mark into my realm. I long to hum to my question mark. I no longer feel enamoured of panko encrusted cod. I desire no panko. I am undesirous of anything to nibble or ingest. Perhaps if just this once you picked me up I would not wish to play put me down now but would greatly enjoy to nestle in that place which is just below your heart.

Yours truly and ever with wisps of happy.

Fifty

Dear friend of my heart. At the end of the day when it's just you and I and the Sister-of-your-Heart who is now the Sister-of-my-Heart, the little lamps are lit, your tum-tums are petted, the light over the front door is turned on to dissuade random thieves and psychopathic murderers and roaming johns. The bottle of wine is opened, the glass poured, the plates are on the table, the TV is on for company. That's when all the secrets come spilling out. I know what I like and what I like to do and there's no one to answer to, except for you and I. It's hard to win an argument with you because you've got the never-ending lives and it is quite a struggle to be heard sometimes, with the Others agitating to find their peace with us. But at the end of the day when it's just you and I, the house is at peace and you like to play. The phone may or may not ring, someone may or may not yell into the answering machine, a book will be read, a list made. Another glass poured and another glass drunk as we wonder what goes on in other homes, busier noisier homes, but ultimately only you and I know the freedom that comes with the solitude at the end of the day, when the bills are paid and the fridge is full and the phone may or may not ring but at least no one is hurting. Thank you for this, friend of my heart. Today I rubbed your tummy fourteen times and you did not bite me. What is wrong? I much prefer when you are behaving as an unnatural nightmare.

Fifty-One

Hi, Great Aunt Biddy. No, lovely. It is not me who is writing you e-mails from your own account. I do not understand anything about hieroglyphics or secret soul names that cats confide in each other. It does now finally make sense about Great Opal's tendency toward hooliganism and theft. She is a he. And a very inconsiderate he, what with not making his balls known before this. I think it was unprofessional of the vet to laugh at your expense, not to mention I'm surprised that a de-balling is more expensive than spaying. It really is too bad that the power of "Delete" doesn't work in the real world. I would have thought it was just a little snip-snip and Bob's-Your-Uncle. I wouldn't go to the expense of changing the décor of her (his) room and canopy bed. I'm sure she (he) is very attached to all of her (his) toys and luxuries and truly appreciates every thing you do. Even if you did receive a mysterious delivery of a live hamster display. I recommend that you delete all your credit card information from your computer as soon as possible. Just saying.

Oh, I have a recipe for panko encrusted cod bites if you want it. It doesn't have to be cod. I've found that just about anything can be panko encrusted.

The great gift of Great Opal is that she sure does keep you on a rigid schedule. You'll never forget to eat or forget when to go to sleep or get up. I don't see why you wouldn't take her to Walmart with you, as a reminder of where you are and why. Dressing her (him) in the coloured kerchiefs with the days of the week written on them is a great idea. It's almost like Great Uncle Beeswax knew all those scarves would have a good use eventually.

Jack is now Great Jack Savage as befits a sailor. He said it just wasn't manly to be forever saddled with having been the miracle baby, especially as he recently won a great battle with a creature he describes as a long-toothed four-legged eel shark. It tried to climb aboard his boat one night but thankfully it was afraid of cats. In particular, it was afraid of Cat.

Fifty-Two

Dearest Keeper of the Lists. Today as we were sun bathing and cleaning our nether regions we meditated upon the burgeoning stack of lists upon the table where we like to nap. Further perusal reveals that each list is almost exactly but not quite like the other. In some way this is similar to how each incarnation is almost never similar to another. In this manner of logic we can then realize that the compulsion to recreate the new list daily to be almost exactly but not quite like another is a form of soul progression similar to but not quite the same as how we ourselves travel through our lives. Do not wither in the face of such minute progress! In a previous life when we were the Beloved Cats of Alcatraz we once witnessed Al Capone dig his way through a concrete wall with a teaspoon. It was truly unfortunate that our own interest in and excitement over the hole led to its discovery by prison officials. Mr. Capone was distinctly hostile toward us thereafter, but I digress within the tantalizing orchards of my marvelous lives.

I would like to procure the live HAMSTER display for Sister-of-my-Heart and would also like to humbly ask why you have deleted your credit card information from the Come-Pewter? Do not worry. Sister-of-my-Heart has a photographic memory and is able to recollect the numbers.

Of late I seem to feel that perhaps our humble abode which we so generously share with you is less than warm enough for my tender tenders. Perhaps this will be rectified with the heating winds which blow through the floors? I also wish for the pleasure of once again looking at my self in the azure waters of the gentle Nile. I dream of the soft ripples that call to me from long ago. I perhaps will increase my sleeping hours to eighteen in the hopes of dreaming such a dream again.

Yours in Splendorous Songs of Stalk and Kill. Welcome forth, O Cleopatra.

Fifty-Three

DEAR BRIDIE SAVAGE. PER YOUR REQUEST FOR IN-FORMATION ON BRINGING ANIMALS, SPECIFICALLY CATS, INTO THE COUNTRY OF SPAIN: YOUR CATS WILL NEED AN APPROVED VETERINARY CERTIFICATE OF GOOD HEALTH. THIS WILL INCLUDE THE IDENTIFICA-TION OF THE OWNER AND THE PERSON RESPONSIBLE FOR THE ANIMALS, DESCRIPTION AND ORIGINS OF THE ANIMALS, MICROCHIP AND/OR TATTOO IDENTI-FICATION OF EACH ANIMAL AND VERIFICATION OF RABIES VACCINE IN COMPLIANCE WITH ALL STAN-DARD INTERNATIONAL REQUIREMENTS. EACH ANI-MAL WILL NEED A PASSPORT AND ALL VISAS ISSUED WILL BE VALID FOR SIX MONTHS FROM THE DATE OF ARRIVAL. WE THANK YOU FOR YOUR INQUIRY AND WISH YOU WELL WITH YOUR VISIT TO OUR BEAUTI-FUL COUNTRY. DO NOT HIT REPLY TO THIS E-MAIL.

Fifty-Four

Dear Eduardo Gonzales. Thank you for the picture of you riding your favourite horse, Diablo. And for the picture of you, Diablo and your mother. And that is one very pregnant barn cat you've got there. Please don't infer anything from the fact that I am sending along pictures of my Great Aunt Biddy, my son Great Jack, my cats, and one of me taken this morning. I know I look a bit tired but it was 5:13 a.m. and my little Nikki seems to have gone off her food. In any case, it isn't the best photo of me, but seeing as we're never going to meet one way or another it is just as well that you see me at my worst and not get to thinking that I'm a beauty queen or anything like that. I also want to apologize for the confusion but it wasn't me who applied for Cat Passports. I mean it was but it wasn't. It's possible that it's me. Or it is possible that there are stranger things in heaven and earth than are dreamed of in any philosophy.

It isn't that I don't want to go to Spain. Especially since of late my own life resembles the Salvador Dali painting *The Persistence of Memory*. Time standing still and dripping all over itself when before everything was rigid and fixed, as if time stood still. I would not be surprised if the plants began to walk around and demand live flies for feeding. I hope not, though.

Diablo is beautiful. I had to Google Andalusians to see exactly what sort they are. A "Cobra" of Andalusians is a sight to behold. I've heard of a "Clowder" of Cats and a "Murder" of Crows, so now I can add "Cobra" to my list. Have I mentioned that I am an obsessed list-maker? When I worked as an actor I wrote my lines out by hand in order to better remember them. A list of lines. Now I write lists of things I need to remember to do each day. A List of Doings. I also write out lists of memories. A List of Remembrances. Memory can be a bit fleeting in my family, or take its own twists and turns along the path to being functional.

Anyway, you look like a very nice man. I think the gold tooth is very charming.

Sincerely yours and it's really too bad we will never get to meet.

Stop hitting reply.

Fifty-Five

Dear Rita. It is wonderful to hear that Mickey has not only learned how to get down from off the top of the cabinet by himself, but he is tightrope walking across the clothesline! Rent him out to Cirque du Soleil. I would very much worry about his newfound interest in lying across the computer keyboard while you are trying to do your work.

Great Uncle Beeswax's most fervent wish upon his eighty-ninth birthday was that he would live just one more year in order to reach 90. Upon achieving that he wished for just one more year and proceeded in that fashion to live to be ninety-four. I think his greatest disappointment in life was that after living to be such a great age he did not win the lottery even once. He thought that the longer one lived the greater the chances. He was hoping to live to be one hundred.

He had a fabulous collection of toilet paper that he won at card games. Giant jumbo packs, most of them not even opened. He always gave me one every time I went to visit. How can a person die with their toilet paper still unopened? It seemed to me a guarantee of immortality, this awareness of toilet paper. You never think that when you open a new pack of toilet paper that you won't live to see the end of it. I still have the feeling that it's bad luck to run out of toilet paper.

His greatest fear was that he was going to have to go into a home where all they fed people was green Jell-o and made people watch *100 Huntley Street* all day long.

Here is what I dreamed last night. Great Uncle Beeswax came to visit. He came in the front door and wandered through the rooms of my house. He spent a long time in the kitchen, gazing at the statue of St. Joseph. Lala was overjoyed to see him and even Great Grandy had a tear in her eye. Beeswax, she said. You're holding up pretty good for a dead fellow.

He said now then now then. This wasn't in the works at all. What have you lot been up to?

He said when I turned ninety the doctor told me, he said, Mr. Beeswax, you've got to slow down. And I told him, my sonny boy, I have made clothing for eight hours straight every day of my life, no matter what, rain or shine or sleet or storm and once during a tsunami. I'm not going to slow down. I'm not going to become lazy simply because I'm ninety. But then it seemed like in a blink I turned ninety-three. It's a queer thing. There were times I felt no good for anything at all. I'd sit down to sew a pair of pants and then find myself standing at the window instead. All I wanted was to live to be a hundred. Yes, see, when I was eighty-nine, I said, I only hope I live to be ninety. But then when I made it to ninety, that felt so good, I thought, I only hope I live to be ninety-one. And when I got to be ninety-one, I said, shag it. I hope I get to one hundred. I never thought I might have to slow down. But then I found that we all will slow down and the only polite thing to do is settle in for the long rest and leave the world to itself. It's only polite.

He said, Bridie, you will always be a Bridie and never should you be anything or anyone else. Always a Bridie is who you should be. Look to St. Joseph. He'll watch over you. You'll be all right.

He took Great Grandy by the hand and she made a great show of putting down *War and Peace* before she patted her hair and rose to take his arm. Lala took up her martini glass as if in defiance but he took up one also and all three fell in step together. He quietly hummed as they walked down the stairs. But what is truly odd is that he stopped to look back at Nikki who then chased after him, her quivering tail up high. She didn't look back.

He did look back, though, once, and winked at me. I tried to wink back but I could never wink. It has to do with the astigmatism. I end up blinking both eyes at once. I waved instead.

I finally got to say goodbye.

FOLKLORISTS DEMAND INQUIRY INTO DISAPPEARANCE OF OLD HAG!

"The Old Hag" has long been blamed for the sleep syndrome in which victims awaken to find they are paralyzed and are infused with a feeling of dread. People for centuries have described awaking in the middle of the night to find an old woman, the Old Hag, sitting on their chest and tormenting them with terrors and evil wishes. All of this activity has suddenly stopped, much to the relief of sufferers. But folklorists are outraged and demand an inquiry into what could have happened to their beloved witch-like muse.

Fifty-Seven

Hi lovely. Thank you for your 17 messages. I have gone over my check list.

It's a good thing I checked the lint trap on the dryer because who knew that so much lint could accumulate just from doing a few loads of laundry? A few dozen loads. That thing was a fire hazard in waiting if ever I've seen one. This then is the hazard of wearing a different outfit each day and taking it off before going to bed and then getting up and putting on something different. It's so much work!

The deadbolt is locked on the front door. I also have added to my list to always double check that I've actually taken the keys from out of the doorknob.

Now I also must admit that I've finally realized that it is not the case that you keep sending me the same emails over and over. It's that I keep forgetting that I've already read them. But it's very interesting that the list is always applicable.

I'm sorry I'm a bit distracted today. Nikki is sleeping all the time. Or I think she's sleeping. She lies very still with one eye open. I'm taking her to the vet. She didn't panic at the sight of the carry cage with the chewed-off lock, so clearly something is wrong. Nishi has emerged from the closet and lies very close by, almost but not quite touching her sister.

Lala and Great Grandy have gone. The house is tidy. My clothes are back in the closet. There are no spectres hovering, pinching or lecturing. But it does feel awfully lonely all of a sudden. Nishi has searched all the closets but the only thing in the closets now are things that ought to be and not things that oughtn't. I know I wished for peace and quiet but why oh why do I continually wish for the wrong things?

WANTED TO BUY: GOAT TESTICLES. PREFERABLY NOT STILL ATTACHED TO THE GOAT. PRECOOKED WOULD BE NICE BUT WILLING TO TAKE GOAT TESTICLES IN ANY WAY SHAPE OR FORM. PRICE IS ABSOLUTELY NO OBJECT AS LONG AS IT IS NOT TOO EXPENSIVE. PLEASE CONTACT BRIDIE SAVAGE AT THE CONTACT INFORMATION LISTED BELOW. URGENT.

Fifty-Nine

But soft! What light through tender heart shines upon my visage? It is good our Muttering Bard did not behold such beauty else he would have written sonnets to end the time of times.

In a previous life when Sister-of-my-Heart and I were Portuguese Long Tails she did inadvertently mistake a wolf's snout for a mouse. The snout was peeking out from beneath a stack of wooden pallets. She did leap upon it and sink her talons deep within. For long these many lives I have perhaps nursed a small resentment toward her because of this. I now do hereby un-nurse this grievance and send it thither and yon.

?

My question mark has at last come to me. She sits upon the chair and rocks gently as I nuzzle her humming curve. She whispers to me of Coronation Street. What is Coronation Street? Is it food? Would it run away if I leapt upon it? Wherefore the preponderance of serial killers upon this street? Wherefore the crock pot was not foretold? O question, how I curl within thine curvature and dream of azure waters wherein my visage peers below as from above.

I am in the way of knowing why thou has been chosen, O heart. Never was one so sublimely suited or well fitted for this task. This miracle is not of mine making, but it was mine loving destiny to follow this thread unto the golden joy.

I leap!

Eulogy for a Cat

Welcome friends. Welcome to our beautiful meadow. Here we stand in a meadow where it is as if nothing ever was, but where something most definitely was. And will be again.

I'm so glad that Great Aunt Biddy and Great Opal finally get to meet my friends. I'm so glad that we have all come together. Wow. It's nice to see Great Opal again. That's very pretty, how the real pearl necklace which I thought one day was going to be mine is now a collar. Also imagine my surprise to find that I am really the change-of-life-miracle illegitimate love child of Great Aunt Biddy and a boyfriend she was engaged to but jilted at the altar. Which makes her my mother, which feels very odd to say, so I'll just stick with Great Aunt Biddy. In this instance it was her who was the runaway love, which is awesome, because I thought it was something that had to happen to us Savages, and not something that could work the other way around.

Great Jack, Sylvia, and their cat named Cat send their regrets, but we will be seeing them very soon.

Welcome Meg and Edgar. Edgar looks great in his fedora. A true great detective feline if ever I met one.

Welcome Rita and Mickey, Moxie and Roxie. I see Mickey is back in his helmet again. It's OK little guy.

Welcome to our new friends Jane and Marilyn. We are glad you could join us. You both were special to Nikki. Marilyn, you're welcome to have all the hors d'oeuvres you like, you don't have to stuff them into your pocket. There are plenty. Sorry, yes, you're right, I will just bladder off but not just yet.

I have one more guest to welcome and may I say how great it is to see you, Hazel, formerly known as the Old Hag. I've got to say I love the crew cut hair with the lavender eye shadow. You'll look perfect when you get your new dentures. Congratulations on your new job as a restaurant hostess/bouncer at Scuzzies Raunchy Bar and Bistro. I can tell that it was you who added the "bistro" part. That really classes up the place.

Welcome to the wake and memorial service for our beloved Great Nikki Savage. Her little kidneys shut down from the side-effects of the steroids we used to treat her OCD. The magic stopped. At the last I filled the bath with water, poured in blue bath salts and held her gently as she peered at her own image. She blinked slowly and serenely and sighed. And that was it. As I gazed into the water with her I caught a glimpse, just for a moment, of a face within my own face. It was both familiar and strange at the same once. Was it that other her Nikki so often referred to? I don't know.

Nishi is being very badly behaved by spitting and attacking our visitors but it has at least roused her from her grief. Also she hates the leash, which is why she is pretending that she can't walk. She is beginning to eat again. At first not even panko encrusted plastic grass could tempt her. The vet says her penchant for plastic is caused by a condition called pica. We have her on a new drug for that but not a drug that could prove toxic. She doesn't mind taking it because it tastes like plastic. For a while the only thing that gave either of us any comfort was for me to sit completely still for two hours and seventeen minutes so she could creep up my legs and sit on my lap. Then she would jump down and we'd do it all over again. It is wreaking havoc on my clothing with all the hooks and rents from her claws but it doesn't matter.

You may or may not be surprised to discover that I've come to realize that I was a seasonal worker. Nothing more. Nothing less. Chasing tourists isn't as dangerous or backbreaking as other seasonal work, such as fishing or picking fruit. Or dealing with perverts. I thought I was a great artist waiting for the world to recognize my worth. But I have come to realize the only worth I truly want is standing here with me today in this meadow.

Nikki once offered to share the weight of grief. How much does grief weigh? I have a recurring dream in which she whispers the secret word for her name in my ear. When I wake up although I can still hear it, I can't remember it. But the amazing thing is that it is her voice, her true voice, her true name, at last.

When I first went away to the School for Gifted Normals I would have been upset to know that by gifted they really meant special, and not special in a good way. And by normal they meant abnormal and all the other things they wouldn't be allowed to say today. The School for Gifted Normals was a failed educational pilot project. It was an open concept teaching module, designed to educate those of us kids that the regular school system didn't know how to handle. I was very happy there. We all were. We didn't have to sit at desks, we didn't have to write exams, we didn't have report cards or grades. We wrote and drew and basically emerged almost but not quite capable of taking on any sort of a proper job.

Long after the school I was diagnosed with extreme near-sightedness. It was that which kept me dreamy and uncom-prehending. Why was I so skilled at reading and writing but unable to grasp mathematics? Because in the former I could hold the books against my nose to read and in the latter I could not see the chalkboard. For the longest time I saw the world through a beautiful blurry haze and it was devastat-ing when I finally got glasses and had to look at things as they really were.

But now I look at things indirectly, never directly. Only looking almost but never directly at a thing is the best way to approach life. I open my eyes, I am here. I close my eyes, I am here. I feel all of you surrounding me. I accept that I am gifted. Gifted by your presence. And that feels normal.

I ask myself, do I love life? Can a person or a creature fall in love with a question mark? Is her final message to ques-tion and question? Perhaps I am the one toppling over the edge. It feels fantastic. The humble honour is mine to have been chosen to be the one to be with them in the first time that they do not depart this incarnation together. I take this responsibility very seriously. I will not let Nishi pine away. I apologize in advance to all the neutered goats. But neuter-ing is not the same as killing and those goat testicles are marinating as I write these words.

In her final fit of energy she took a giant leap from the chair to where the statue of St. Joseph sat upon the shelf. She pushed him over the edge and lay down to watch as he fell to the floor and shattered into pieces. Inside was a year's worth of pre-played Lotto tickets, tucked inside by Great Uncle Beeswax. They were all the same numbers, the birth dates and ages of myself, Great Jack and Great Aunt Biddy. The winning ticket was the sixth one in the sequence.

I waited and waited for her ghost to come around, but it never did.

Marilyn was kind enough to share with me what was embroidered inside the leopard skin coat. I've put the words together with some other words we've found and written them down in what might be almost but not quite the correct order. So I will close with these words from Great Uncle Beeswax.

Room of lost stitches
The most impossible plank
Bends with gentle gaze.

Oh and by the way, Marilyn. It's not that I mind you borrowing my purple dress with the hand embroidered pink polka dots but I hung it on the line to dry not for you to take.

Sixty-One

DEAR BRIDIE SAVAGE. CONGRATULATIONS ON THE ACCEPTANCE OF YOUR "ODE TO A CABBAGE". OUR READING COMMITTEE WAS UNANIMOUS. WE WILL BE IN TOUCH SOON WITH A CONTRACT. SINCERELY, THE NEW YORKER MAGAZINE. IF YOU WISH ANY MORE IN-FORMATION PLEASE HIT "REPLY" AND WE WILL BE HAPPY TO REPLY.

Sixty-Two

My Dear Eduardo Gonzales. I have but one question to ask of you: Do you love life? Sincerely, Great Bridie Savage.

Sixty-Three

Dear Bridie Savage. Shannon Tweed has broken her leg in a tragic but non-life threatening freak accident when her dog became entangled in his leash while chasing a cat which mysteriously appeared on her property. We hope you still remember your lines from your recent audition for *The Monarchs* and can step in to help us out? The role has been rewritten to be a recurring character, that of one Cleosandra Hexador, a mysterious aunt who can transform at will into a Painted Lady Butterfly. We will be happy to pay you double scale plus per diem. Please hit reply as soon as possible!

Sixty-Four

dingiblzivng.

mxzibnible!

!!!

hello.

hello?

hellohellohellohellohello.

thisisthecatwholivesherewiththeothercat. butnowlivesherewithouttheothercat.

sister gone. gone sister gone to sweet dreams place to dream of next life. weep cry so sad too sad want to be gone with sister.

but now have message from sister in my heart our heart one heart. sister is already in next life!

we go get her now please and also she say we have another sister so now there will be the cat who lives here with the other cat and one other cat too.

in spain.

also we want fish.

Sixty-Five

Dear Service Canada.

I'm hitting reply one last time to let you know that Nishi and I will be out of the country for an indefinite period of time. In case you miss me. The interesting thing is that if I were still receiving EI from you I wouldn't be allowed to leave the country. Or the city or the province for that matter. Because it is considered that people who receive EI sit around all day long doing nothing anyway so why would they need a restful holiday like any other regular person? I question.

?

Ha!

My jiggles where I wiggle are from where I gave birth to my son Great Jack Savage (formerly known as Jack-the-Miracle-Baby) and are therefore precious. He and his girl Sylvia are going to meet me at the Port of Vigo. Eduardo and his mother are joining us there and although she and he both have the same unibrow, I figure anyone who likes cats that much can't be too terrifying. Great Aunt Biddy who is really my mother is coming also, along with Great Opal. She says looking at the empty meadow where the old homestead stood makes her lonely so why not go look at something else. We buried Nikki there next to Blackie and now there are wild roses growing madly from both graves.

I recollect a fable from long ago about an elephant (Olyfaunt) that fell in love with a firefly. The elephant was so secure in this love that it firmly believed that wherever the firefly went, at the centre of its light was always the image of an elephant.

We put a small marker there, where nothing was before, a branch we found curved along the top, a question mark grown free and wild.

It was difficult getting the travel papers for Great Opal because immigration refused to believe she was a plain old housecat. The vet had to come up with specially notarized travel papers upon which he lied. Great Opal is part lynx and part ocelot, and it just goes to show the danger of adopting exotic animals as house pets and letting them run wild when they get too difficult to handle.

My crinkles where I wrinkle are from being still alive and not dead. My boobs are still on the good side of perky and not too much on the downward-facing-dog side. I have a Buddha belly, a built-in source of wisdom, because we should all listen to our gut. The girl at the salon who trims my hair spends hours and hours dyeing her hair the same shade of silver grey as mine. The most beautiful women I know shine glory out of their eyes and have knowing in their heart.

Jane and Marilyn and Hazel (formerly know as the Old Hag) have moved into my house on Monastery Lane. My worst fear has come true. I am at last the notorious cat lady, proprietor of the first hopefully soon to be legal Cat House of the city. A Cat House that takes in cats, of course. Hookers who want to leave "the life" as they call it, can retrain as veterinary helpers and live in free of charge.

I have a new job waiting for me when I get back. I won the lottery, true, but not millions and millions. I won seventy-eight thousand dollars. Exactly enough to feel like a million bucks, let me tell you. So after the trip, which is my big splurge for us all, I begin my writer-in-residency program at the local community centre. I'm offering a creative writing course called Haiku with Harlots. I pitched the community centre on it using some of Uncle Beeswax's poetry. It doesn't pay very much but it'll keep us in cat food. And it's part of our ongoing initiative to help those ladies of the evening leave the evenings and come out into the light of day.

I got rid of the old answering machine because we all have cellphones now, which is fantastic. I still don't answer the phone, of course, it's the texting which is the wonderful thing. No one has to yell into anything to get my attention.

My yoga is progressing wonderfully. I have moved from Corpse Pose into Sukasana, otherwise known as Easy Pose, or Sitting Up Pose. This involves the art of sitting up without lying down for safety. It's pretty funny. I was sitting on my yoga mat with my eyes closed almost but not quite thinking of anything in particular. A song came from my lips, loud and strong and completely off key. It seems I am tone deaf. I felt a salty breeze upon my face and I levitated while hearing someone play an accordion very badly.

In the centre of my light there is an image of her. I do believe she is there, waiting. We will find her and the other one there with her and I don't know what will happen after that. After Great Uncle Beeswax died I was afraid our patchwork quilt would unravel and that would be the end of us. It turns out we have added to our quilt. It's a lopsided crazy makes no sense kind of quilt, stitched with stitches from out of time.

So, dear friend, and by dear friend I mean you the individual and not you the entity (and by entity I do mean evil demon) I bid you farewell and wish you all the best. If you ever feel you would like to leave "the life" there at Service Canada, and if you have a fondness for cats and other creatures, come find us at Monastery Lane.

Sincerely, Bridie Savage.

Please do not hit reply to this email.

OLD HAG ORGANIZES HOOKERS IN GIANT PROTEST AGAINST OIL BARONS!

The Old Hag is funding the legal battles ahead through the royalties from the wildly popular new app called Cat Scramble. The residents of Monastery Lane say that while they are not happy about the recently opened Cat House in their midst it is much better than the daycare which was previously proposed by the city.

ODE TO A CABBAGE

O tender curling inward

Guarding close your heart

Curving soft

Holding dear your secret

Peel away

Peel away

O tender curling inward

So close in intention to a rose

But not a rose

Or even an artichoke.

ACKNOWLEDGEMENTS

Thank you to Donna Francis and all and sundry at Creative Books Publishing who were involved in birthing this baby. Donna is confidence-inducing and so certain of what she wants, one can't help but feel the glow of being in good and caring hands. It feels exactly like being picked first for the team when you are a kid in school, something that never ever happened to me because I was always picked last, so, Donna, this more than makes up for that. Pam Dooley, thank you for all the tiny details. Pam Frampton, thank you for your eagle eyes.

I want to thank Iain McCurdy for being my editor. He led the way through the maze with a trail of bread-crumbs and a ball of yarn, not the way out of the maze, but deeper within, which is where I needed to go. He is generous with his ideas, and with his support for the tender creations of fragile writers.

Thank you to my readers and friends, Amy House and Marilyn Mackay, who peruse everything I write, even when I hound them to do it, for sharing the beauty of Salmon Cove and huge meals and wine and the beach and all the creatures.

Thank you to Fabian and Shannon and Bristol for being my family by proxy.

Thank you to Sharon King-Campbell and Alix Reynolds and Sherri Levesque for being inspiring young women, for being present, generous, and all around good company.

Most especially I want to acknowledge Boss and Pop, Jonathan and his girl Sarah, and all the members of our family on all sides. The Stapletons and the Butlers are a kind and loving and magical clan.

Nikki&Nish, thank you for being the mysterious enigmatic silly natural born killers that you are.

Thank you to the Newfoundland and Labrador Arts Council and whoever sat on the jury on that particular session on that particular day because when that little envelope arrives in the mail with that little bit of good news it's as good as gold to a struggling writer.

At the end of yoga we thank ourselves for being present on the mat, for having taken this one hour out of this one day to tend to our spiritual and bodily health, so I would like to conclude by thanking me for always being there for me, for never giving up on me and for ultimately being me after all.

ABOUT THE AUTHOR

Berni Stapleton is a Newfoundland-Labrador writer and performer of unique distinction. She is a past recipient of the WANL award for best work in non-fiction for her contribution to the book They Let Down Baskets. Her short stories and essays have appeared in Riddle Fence and The Newfoundland Quarterly. She is a recipient of the Ambassador of Tourism award from Hospitality NL. She lives as she writes, celebrating the extraordinary within the ordinary, believing that everyone should have a Playwright-in-Residence in the house. Just in case.

Upcoming...

This is the Other Cat

The Unity-Verse appears at last to be unfolding in dazzling pleats of good-good for Bridie Savage and her ménage of a family. This means it is exactly the time for all best laid plans to defect to parts unknown, leaving Bridie and her clan of Savages stranded in Spain. A new cat magic is at play, ruthless, teasing, tormenting, bent upon the reunion of two cat soul sisters, which goes terribly, comically, awry.

Meow